LAURIE LEE

Once Upon a Time in Fairyland

Laurie Lee

ISBN: 978-1-0881-7166-0

Contents

.

Rumpelstiltskin

(previously self-published as Creating Gold,
now expanded and revised)

The origin of Rumpelstiltskin is German. Tales were told as early as the 16th century. It was in 1812 that the Brothers Grimm wrote it as part of their collection of household tales. In the original tellings, Rumpelstiltskin was some type of a goblin. In my retelling, he is something quite different. Happy reading!

Chapter 1

Sebastian Mornn, Chancellor to the king, observed the smoke-drenched common room of the Wayside Inn where he'd been forced to stop. Pouring rains continued beating against the slated roof, bringing more drenched, unwashed bodies into the crowded room. His favored jacket would have to be burned. Anger simmered beneath his quiet surface as he studied the denizens surrounding him.

A fly buzzed along a trail of rotten meat, landing on a heavy oak table. Air stirred and a heavy fist flattened the insect. Another man dropped his hand of cards in the center of the circle of players. Shouts rose as a queen of spade skid across the table. A large man tipped his chair and another player's arm swung into him. He fell back, his howl of anger disrupting the general cadence of the room. Laughter burst through the air.

Noise abated in a moment. The game continued and Sebastian frowned into his empty mug. He smoothed a crease from his black shirt as he waved to the buxom blonde for more drink. The flicker of fear in her eyes made him smirk. A pleasure it was, to have power.

"Aye, a talented lass for sure."

Another conversation nabbed his attention. He turned his gaze to a thin man lifting a glass of wine. His mode of dress suggested a pauper gentleman.

"Nothing compared to my daughter." A different man slapped the table, his grin wide. "The elder, mind you. Now there's a lass who'll turn flax to gold."

Narrowing his eyes, Sebastian assessed the braggart making a fool of himself. Nondescript, save for a decorated jacket inlaid with golden strands. The hair on his neck tickled. *What manner of man devised such tales of his kin?* Sebastian stroked his goatee. As night settled and fires were laid in the grates to ward off the chill, the king's Chancellor crafted a fine scheme to fill the dull winter months at the palace.

LAURIE LEE

Chapter 2

Elizabeth Haddock stared at the card causing her father to squeal boorishly. A symbol of the king's emblem had been etched in a silver plate. She turned it over, but there was nothing more. She looked at her father. "What does it mean?"

"It is an invite to the Palace a fortnight from today."

Shocked, Elizabeth flipped the card again. "Invited to the palace? Where does it say such a thing?"

"Not on the card." Her father, Benner Haddock, nabbed it from her. "The servant told me. A fortnight. From today. Caroline and I are invited to stay at the palace for a winter gathering."

Elizabeth looked over the dusty, old furniture against the walls of the morning room. And this was the nicest of their rooms. "Why would the king invite you to the palace?"

Her father shrugged. "Caroline is much sought after. She is a beauty, you know. Why shouldn't the king have heard of her?" He tucked the precious card in his pocket and grabbed Elizabeth by the hands. He began to twirl her around the room. "Your sister shall dance with royalty, my dear. She will dazzle him. I've always known it."

Elizabeth skipped her feet to keep up with her father as her mind whirled with danger. "But should you go? We aren't exactly in kilter with his usual ilk."

With a credulous cry, her father released her. Elizabeth stumbled backward, managing to catch her balance before falling to the threadbare carpet.

"Not go?" His eyes appeared to fill with horror. "Are you daft, child? Caroline not go to the king? She will captivate him. He will fall in love and marry her. Would you deny your sister the opportunity of happiness and wealth beyond imagining?"

"Of course not, Father." Elizabeth tucked her hair behind her ear. "But the king is not known for kindness toward young ladies."

He waved away her concern. "He is not likely to harm her with her father present."

Elizabeth opened her mouth for further protest, but an angry darkness hardened her father's face. Remaining silent, she stepped back and swallowed as he leaned closer.

"Disgrace and envy flow from your lips, daughter, and I will not have it. Depart from me, I want no more of your presence today." He pulled the card from his pocket and turned from her.

Elizabeth blinked tears from her eyes as she took the back set of stairs to her room. "I must warn Caro."

A tray laden with food arrived at her room before she finished dressing for supper. The kitchen worker offered a weak smile, placed the tray on a dresser near the window, and left her alone. Her heart grew heavy as she realized her father did not want to see her at the dining table.

Hours later, Elizabeth heard someone moving through the room beside hers. She rushed into the hallway and knocked on her sister's door. Caroline greeted her with a mocking grin and a shake of her head. Where Elizabeth was short and slender, Caroline stood tall and graceful. Her golden hair cascaded down her back as she pulled pins from the coiffure.

"Really, Lizzie." Her sister's gray eyes sparkled with teasing. "You told Father I should not meet the king? He supposes you to be jealous, but what is there to be jealous of?" She waved her hand. "His royal highness would never notice a little thing like you. How often have I told you, you lack presence?"

"But Caro, such a man." Elizabeth ignored the usual taunts and sat on the bed, leaning against one of the posters as she tucked one leg beneath her. Though less than two years older, Caroline's glance caused Elizabeth to feel like a scolded child. She faced downward and plucked at her dressing gown.

Caroline opened the double doors of her wardrobe. "Of course, I must go, silly girl. I will meet the king. We will dance, he and I." She rummaged through the gowns.

"You believe him to be an honorable man?"

Frowning, her sister sent her a sharp glance. "Honorable? He is our king. Why should I be concerned if he is honorable? Power suits me more than honor."

"He is not like the boys in town, Caro. You

cannot toy with him as you do the others."

Head shaking, Caroline stepped away from her perusal and pulled Elizabeth to her feet. She guided her to the door with a firm hand against her elbow. Elizabeth sighed.

Caroline's eyes rebuked as sharply as her words. "You've a simple mind, my dear. When I am queen, I will invite you to the palace where you are sure to be a novelty."

"Don't go." Elizabeth tried one last time. For a moment, Caroline's eyes revealed doubt. But then she shook her head and ushered Elizabeth through the door.

"You will see, Lizzie. A great man is permitted to love. He is bound to marry someone, why not me?"

The door closed firmly, leaving Elizabeth alone in the dimly lit hallway. Heaviness tightened her chest and clogged her throat as she returned to her bedroom. Their minds were set, and one thing remained.

Entering her own room offered no comfort. A small fire burned in the grate, causing shadows to flicker against the walls. Her bed mirrored Caroline's, her dresser and stand elegantly gleaming, though she knew most of the clothes within were patched and worn. Sobbing, she sank to her knees beside the bed. Father had spoken frequently of the king's exploits with disdain. How could he agree to attend? Caroline she could understand, but Father? Tears dampened her cheek.

"God. I don't understand why I have such fear in my heart. Oh please, send someone to protect them. Let them not fall into danger. I shake at the thought of their going, though I know not why. Help them please, Lord. Protect them."

Cold seeped through her nightgown and she crawled beneath the covers of her bed. Prayers drifted through her mind until sleep claimed her.

~

The feel of smooth wood beneath his fingers gave Rumpelstiltskin a sense of accomplishment. Hours of sanding following days of carving were worth the effort.

"Rom."

He turned at the sound of his name being called. A moment later, his friend entered the workshop at the back of a barn. "What has you out and about, Olsome?"

"Searching for you. What's the prince doing in a worn-out barn?"

Rom lifted one brow. "The space was good enough for my grandfather."

"Your grandfather has a journey for you."

Rom stood. "For me?"

"Don't—"

Rom didn't wait to hear more. He thought of his grandfather and then allowed his mind to take him there.

Alforstiltzkin looked up from the ledger on his desk as Rom appeared. He frowned. "I would caution against your talent, but I think it may come in handy."

"Why is that?" Rom was used to being able to appear and disappear at will.

"Our High King has revealed someone in need.

You are the means to help."

"My father approves?"

Grandfather's lip twitched. "The king recognizes the power that is greater than he. He will not keep you from this destiny."

Rom rubbed his hands together. "We are Guardians for our High King. I am excited to learn more."

Grandfather leaned back. "It will involve creating gold."

Rom sat to hear more.

Chapter 3

The last vestige of light turned the sky deep burgundy. Caroline paused at the window to stare across rolling hills dotted with trees. A loon called through the growing darkness. Excitement buzzed through her as she pulled the heavy curtains and faced her guestroom within the palace. Whinmoore Palace. She was really here. Though the housekeeper's servant who brought her to the room claimed it as one of the smallest, the room was larger than what she knew from home. Blue paper with gilded birds covered the top half of the walls. The bottom half was painted lighter blue. A large bed with dark wood posts took up most of the main room, though there was a straight-backed chair and round table near the window.

A second room held her clothes, most of those newly purchased. She also had her own indoor bathroom. What a lovely luxury. The maid promised to draw a bath for her in the mornings after breakfast. But for tonight… she twirled. Dinner, perhaps dancing.

A knock sounded at the door, pulling Caroline from exploring the opulent room. A small ladies maid entered. "Good evening, mum. I've been sent to help you prepare for this evening."

Caroline nodded and offered a tight smile. "I appreciate the attention."

The young maid helped her don a rose underlay with a crimson skirt and matching vest that buttoned up the front. The sleeves of the underlay ballooned at her upper arms and gathered with thick lace. The maid tugged on the back of the vest. "You look charming."

Caroline straightened her shoulders as she studied herself in the mirror. Her dark hair was piled on her head except for a long strand over her left shoulder that had been twisted into a curl. She'd thought the color of the gown too rich for a young woman, but with her dark hair and pale skin, she felt resplendent. Her green eyes shone. "You may fetch a lad to take me to the parlor where guests gather."

The maid bowed and left. Caroline pressed her hands against her belly. In a matter of moments, she would meet King Hewel. She was determined he would not forget her.

Another knock on the door and Caroline found herself looking up at a man more important than a palace servant.

"Forgive the intrusion." He bowed. "I am Chancellor Mornn. It would be my pleasure to escort you to our gathering."

She lowered her gaze. "Thank you. I appreciate your attention." Though she did not recognize him, his long blue jacket with gold buttons, as well as the thin circlet of gold on his head, marked him as one of great importance.

"I have been looking forward to tonight's

party," he said as they walked the hallway.

"Is there something of significance?"

"I think the king has a plan. I would not wish to spoil it for him."

"Indeed, not." Caroline felt her heart swell within her.

Their chatter remained unimportant as he guided her through the labyrinth of halls and stairs until they reached a large room buzzing with people.

"Ah, my daughter." Her father called to her.

Chancellor Mornn bowed. "A pleasure, my lady."

Then he left her.

Father watched him leave. "Who was that?"

Caroline squeezed his hands. "Chancellor to the king. He personally led me from my chambers."

Father smiled as his chest puffed. "An honor."

Caroline gazed across the magnificent room. Chandeliers with crystal forms shone above the gathering like heavenly lights. "I shall have to write Lizzie."

"Don't waste time with that silly girl. You have more important things to attend." He took her hand for a moment. "Enjoy your night. Charm King Hewel. There is nothing else you need bother about."

Once he released her hand, he gave her a wide smile and then sauntered off.

"A glass of wine?" A servant offered, holding a silver tray with a goblet. His face was down. Caroline felt a burn of pleasure at the gesture of humbleness. She took the glass and moved away. More people entered. A palette of colors added to the festive atmosphere. Somewhere, a clock struck and the air itself seemed charged with excitement. A cord of trumpeters sounded. Caroline turned along with everyone else.

A set of oversized doors opened. Soldiers entered first, taking places at intermittent points along the walls. Then came half a dozen servants wearing gold uniforms, making them stand out from any others. An older woman with silver hair was carried in a litter. Most everyone's attention followed the king's mother, but Caroline was more interested in King Hewel. She longed for her first glimpse of him. The man did not disappoint. He entered, followed by Chancellor Mornn. Though the king was not as tall, his wide shoulders and thick chest made him appear larger. His dark hair was thick, with a slight curl. The tone of the metal in his crown seemed to have been chosen to complement his hair. His face tightened as he first peered through the crowd of people. Elizabeth's warning about him being a difficult man seeped into her mind, but she willed it away. There was more than romance involved here.

She watched as the chancellor introduced him to a sallow-faced girl with too many ruffles in her skirt. The two men followed by four of the servants wandered among the people, stopping to chat with some. Ignoring others. Caroline chatted with an older couple, although she kept her attention on the nearing pair. When they finally joined them, she turned.

Chancellor Mornn grinned. "Here is the beauty I escorted to our gathering. Miss Caroline, I believe."

Caroline dipped graciously, and then gazed up at King Hewel. His vivid blue eyes caused flutters within her stomach.

"A pleasure." He greeted.

Caroline tilted her head but said nothing.

King Hewel narrowed his gaze. "What?"

She waved her hand. "Some silly response."

His lips twitched with amusement. "I give you leave to speak your mind."

Caroline raised her chin. "You did not seem pleased when you first saw the crowd awaiting you."

He laughed. "I sent my mother with all the pomp she could desire so I might enter unobtrusively."

"You should not invite so many people if you do not care for a crowded room."

"Some events require pomp and ceremony, though I prefer more... intimate occasions."

Chancellor Mornn led him onward, and Caroline pressed her hand against her chest. She had done it. He would remember her.

~

Caroline sipped wine and flirted with a young man at her left elbow. Surreptitious glances toward the king revealed his attention. She waited until his eyes almost met her own, and then lowered her lashes and caused her cheeks to pinken. She lifted a silver fork to her lips, though she knew not what she tasted. Her attention fixed on the lush room with carved sconces and painted ceiling. The walls above the chair rails were a medley of colors subtly swirled together, perfect backdrop for paintings of plump nudes.

The king's table sat thirty patrons, and the din garbled her partner's words. She smiled prettily and nodded when she thought she should. Course after course was placed before her and removed by silent servants. Finally, the king's mother stood. The women placed their lap covers across the table. Caroline followed suit. She joined the line leading away from the dining hall and glanced back toward His Majesty. He lifted his glass and their eyes seemed to meet across the growing distance. Her heart skipped, but she allowed only a small smile to grace her face. She acknowledged him and turned forward.

The palace wormed its way into her heart. Dragging her fingers along a polished redwood rail, she envisioned herself dressed more splendidly than any woman currently present. She accepted the ornately carved chair one of the attendants indicated. With her back straight and crimson skirt settled about her legs, she knew the king's attention would be drawn to her the instant he entered the room. Voices of ladies twitted like birds. Though acquainted with a few, Caroline was intimate friends with no one. She sat, holding herself still, waiting for the gentlemen to join them. Not half an hour had passed when a servant opened the doors to the drawing room, allowing the men to enter.

The king walked the perimeter of the room, his hands clasped behind his back. He spoke a moment with men and women alike, and then moved forward once more. It was in this manner he arrived at Caroline's side. Looking up, she drank in the sight of him. Wide shoulders, square jaw, high forehead. Hard eyes the color of slate. She shivered. His hand stretched toward her, and she felt power in his touch.

"Dinner pleased you?" His voice murmured, this conversation for the two of them only.

"How could it not? Your chef is a master." Caroline felt her heart pound as his hand continued to hold hers.

"I hold quality in high regard."

"Your palace must be rife with masterpieces."

"Would you care to see some?"

The king offered a special tour. She had to quell the giddy excitement that bubbled in her veins. "But what of your other guests?"

He tucked her hand at his elbow and drew her across the room. Apparently, they did not matter. She floated beside him, barely taking note of the gilded rooms they passed, the marble floors they crossed, nor the carved stairs they climbed.

One painting, among a sea of his relatives caught her eye. The sad countenance of the woman leapt from the canvas.

"I, too, am moved by her." The king remained at her side.

"A talented artist, to capture such emotion." Caroline sounded awed.

"I relish talent. Craftsmen of quality are a rarity in these modern times."

Caroline studied the king. This close, she could see feathers of silver cascading from his temples. His hair waved around his ears and touched the collar of his dress shirt. The velvet vest pulled tight across his chest, and she doubted padding had been needed to adjust the fit. He stood a head taller than herself, allowing her eyes to rest on the golden medallion he wore around his neck. Lost in perusal, she hadn't realized he'd been talking. She looked up as a question registered.

"Are you?"

Caroline blinked. "Am I?"

"A master weaver?"

Her mouth widened with pleasure. "You do not require false modesty, do you, Sire?" At the shake of his head, she leaned closer. "I am known throughout my village."

"Who taught you?"

"My mother. Hers was a talent that could sparkle in twilight."

"Your father made an interesting claim. Caught the attention of Chancellor Mornn." The king led her into the hallway and up a flight of stairs. Caroline warmed to his particular attention. Dreams of living in the palace filled her mind.

They stopped at the first door to a wing of offices. She blushed when she saw the grand bed against the far wall. But then she noticed a mound of plant material and an old spinning wheel. She pointed. "What is plant debris doing inside the palace?"

"That is the flax you will spin into gold."

Caroline laughed, turning away. "Spin into gold? What an odd tease you are."

He stopped her with a firm hand on her arm. "Your father has claimed it is possible. You yourself claim to be talented."

"At weaving. With cotton or silk even. But this? How is such a thing to be achieved?"

The king's manner cooled. He distanced himself with arms crossed over his chest. "And yet, that is your task. You will spin the flax into gold by morning light, or you will die."

The king pushed her into the room. She stood in the bare space in the center of the bedroom as he offered a brief bow and closed the door. And clicked a lock. And a second lock. She stared, waiting. Surely, he meant to return. To joke at his clever humor? Silence dragged.

The walls offered no windows. She walked to the door and pulled. It refused to budge. Fear set in. She walked to the mound of flax and lifted a piece. The thin flat leaf was nearly as long as her arm. She looked at the spinning wheel. Was one piece even big enough to go through the machine? How would it work? Her chest began to quiver with sobs as she held the piece of leaf against the wood of the spindle, and then the wheel. Where was one to put it? Even if she could figure that, how could a plant become gold thread?

Despair overwhelmed her. She threw herself onto the bed with a howl.

"That's not going to help much, is it?"

Caroline screamed, rolled to the far side of the bed, and held a pillow to her chest.

A slender man, shorter than herself, stood near the door. His flamboyant yellow jacket and slacks lit the room with color. His eyes sparkled with mischief.

Though her heart still pounded, she found she could not fear him. Something about him set her at ease. She scooted closer, still clinging to the pillow.

"Why is maiden fair sobbing her heart upon the bed?" he asked with an elegant bow.

Caroline stood. She shuddered as she took a deep breath. "The king has set an impossible task. I will die when morning comes."

"Travesty." He pressed his hand to his heart, eyes widened with horror. "The king is a fool. What task has milady been charged with?"

Caroline pointed at the fresh mound of plant cuttings. More tears dripped down her cheeks.

"And the king wants?" His raised brows revealed his need and desire for more information.

"Gold. From that." She could barely say the words.

"Ah." The man nodded. He rubbed his hand over his chin. "A daring dream indeed. You are loved, dear girl, by powers great and true. For I have come."

"To help me?" Caroline wasn't sure how anyone could help.

"If that is your wish."

Caroline didn't hesitate. She released the pillow and crossed the room. She unclasped a silver necklace and placed it in his hand.

He took a step back, as though surprised. He looked at his hand and then at her face.

"I wish it." Caroline rushed. She grabbed a handful of flax, selected a wide piece, and handed it to him. The stranger stood for a moment, one hand holding the leaf and the other clasping her necklace. With a shrug, he slipped the necklace into a front pocket and sat behind the wheel. He placed his feet on two boards near the floor. With a push, the wheel began to spin. He fed the flax through the guide, and then looked at her with his hand stretched out.

Caroline barely noticed. She watched the spokes blur as they spun. The machine seemed to shimmer. She startled when he stopped. "What are you doing?"

He gave her an odd glance. "I'm going to need more materials."

"But what has happened to the first?"

"Take a look for yourself." He nodded at the bobbin where the fiber was stored. Caroline stepped closer. Against the wood shaft of the spool lay a yarn the color of gold. She touched it, uncertain her eyes didn't deceive her. But the yarn felt smooth and metallic.

She didn't realize he'd crossed the room until he dumped a pile of leaves at her feet and sat down. Sweeping her skirts out of the way, she watched his legs begin to move and the wheel to spin. Joy surged through her. She danced across the bedroom, grabbing the pillow once more. With a contented sigh, she flopped onto the bed. Relief filled her. She was saved. Stretching, she imagined the king's surprise on the morrow. His delight. In her. Thoughts of grandeur and the sound of the wheel spinning around and around lulled her to sleep.

Pounding on the door woke her. She sat with a start in the dark, and then yelped as the door opened and slammed against the wall. Light poured into the chamber. With a gasp of fright, Caroline looked to the center of the room where the wheel sat. No sign of the slender man remained. She twisted around to look at the pile of flax, but only a few crumbs remained on the floor. The other wall was stacked with bobbins thick with golden thread. She raised triumphant eyes to the king and his chancellor.

~

Elizabeth flipped through the letters newly arrived. An invitation to a ball, but nothing from

Father or Caro. She sighed. Could they not at least let her know they arrived safely?

She sat on the bench beneath the hall window. It was winter, so there were no leaves rustling on the trees. Gray skies gave everything a gloomy air. Was this to be her lot? Tucked away, only cared for by servants? "Please, God," she whispered as she pressed her hand against a windowpane. "Help Caro and help me."

A red bird fluttered to the ground a few feet from where she sat. Its vivid color shone like a beacon on the dull day. Watching it flip through dead leaves to forage for food gave Elizabeth hope.

~

That night, King Hewel celebrated. A grand hall had been transformed with tables and benches. To Caroline, it seemed hundreds made merry as minstrels sang and flautists played. She and her father sat beside the king, upon a raised dais. The chancellor and several princes ate with them. Caroline barely noticed the thick herbed lamb shank filling her plate. The king held her attention. His eyes enthralled her, their deep blue color warm and inviting. She could not resist accepting his hand as he stood.

"What part of the castle would you desire to see tonight?" His deep voice caused butterflies to flutter in her stomach.

"I do not have enough knowledge of the palace to make a choice, Sire."

"My name is Aaden." He lifted her hand to his lips.

Caroline debated if swooning would be a proper

reaction, but she didn't want to miss a moment of her time with the king, with Aaden. He led her to an upper hall. They toured a set of rooms known for their color: peacock, amber, crimson, emerald, and jade. It wasn't until they had travelled up and down multiple sets of stairs that he opened one last door. Her breath caught in her throat when she saw the mound of greenery, twice the size of the previous night. She straggled to back away from the door, but he thrust her into the room.

"Serve me with your rare talent, and I will honor you exceedingly. Fail me, and you will die at morning's light."

She turned, grasping his arm with desperation. "Sire, it is too much, too soon. Aaden, I cannot."

He pulled her fingers from him. "You will. Or you die." He closed the door, and she heard locks engaging once more.

Caroline cried. Desperation overwhelmed her and she fell across the bed.

"Terrible sounds from such a lovely lady."

She sat up without a hiccup. The odd little man stood at the door. Today his coat and pants were green, set off by a white shirt and crafted tie. Several fingers were wrapped with thin strips of fabric, but Caroline did not care.

"You've come to help with the new challenge," she rushed to him, falling to her knees as she grasped his hands.

"If that is your wish."

She dug a leather pouch from a hidden pocket in her evening gown. She had lifted it from her father in case the need arose. She tossed it to the stranger. He bounced it once in his hand and then it disappeared.

Caroline flopped onto the soft bed with a sigh of contentment. The sound of spinning filled the room, and she allowed it to lull her to sleep.

~

"Here is your third challenge, my lady. Succeed this evening and I will make you my queen. Fail me and you die in the morning light."

She had expected it this time, but the sight of the tremendous mound of flax caused her heart to pound. She muffled her cries into the feathered pillow.

"My heart breaks for you, sweet lady. Is nary a night of peace your fate?"

Caroline rushed to his side, barely able to contain her excitement. "He has promised marriage. One final night, but I have nothing to offer you for your service."

"If you are to be queen, I am sure you could think of something."

Caroline couldn't help but think of the gorgeous gowns that would fill her closets. The dainty shoes that would cover her feet. And jewels. Mounds of jewels would make her rich beyond imagining. She cast a sly eye at her savior. There was nothing in her thoughts from which she would be willing to part.

"I have a sister," Caroline brightened. "She could be a great help for you. She is simple, but kindhearted. It is a perfect plan. I am certain she will adore you." Caroline didn't wait for his response. She picked up an armful of flax and dropped it by the spinning wheel. Exhausted by her night of dancing, she fell across the bed and slept.

Chapter 4

After days of quiet, the noise of a carriage in the lane grabbed Elizabeth's attention. She stood to peer through a window. "They've returned," she declared, clasping her hands and hurrying to the front of the house. A servant stood ready to open the door. Elizabeth waited, tugging at her hands. As the sound of a knock, she motioned to the servant. "Open, please."

But it wasn't her sister nor her father at the door. She frowned. "What…"

"Greetings, good lady. I carry a letter for Miss Elizabeth."

Though the young man was obviously a servant, he dressed more richly than herself. She rubbed a nervous hand on her simple muslin dress. "I am she."

"Perfect." He held an envelope embossed with gold toward her. "I am to await a response."

Elizabeth frowned as she walked away, turning the elegant missive over. When she reached the east sitting room, she sat at the narrow desk and used a letter opener to break the seal. There was only one page.

My dear Lizzie, though I have only been away

these few weeks, I find I am missing your quiet presence more than I imagined. Please do not deny me the pleasure of your company even though I have come to this place against which you have strong objections.

The carriage will wait for your response. If you are agreeable, you will travel in the height of luxury to join me here. Yours, etc.

And that was it. Nothing about Father, nor how her visit to the king's court progressed. Her first inclination was to refuse. What purpose could she serve in a royal court? She closed her eyes. *I don't want to do this.*

But it is where you must head.

Such a strange letter. The fact remained, Caro called for her. Needed her. At least, Elizabeth hoped she needed her. Elizabeth rang the bell for the housekeeper.

The tall woman looked down her nose.

Elizabeth swallowed. "The servant from the carriage, let him know I will accompany him. I will need a trunk packed."

"Sir Haddock said nothing of you leaving us."

"Caroline wishes me to join them. Please make the necessary arrangements."

She nodded. "We shall."

Preparations took a few hours, but Elizabeth finally arranged a pillow at her back as she settled into the carriage. Though the carriage was not large, it held more creature comforts than she'd ever beheld. She could not feel a board beneath where she sat, yet no sagging in the cushions. The gentle rocking did not jar her or cause her to drop the book of poetry she carried.

She watched the familiar village and hillside give way to unfamiliar forests and farmlands. The sun moved towards its evening rest when they stopped.

After a knock on the door, the young man greeted her with a nod. "You will want to stay here for the night."

Elizabth gripped her pelisse as heat infused her cheeks. "I have no means…"

"Your room has already been requested. You will find a maid waiting for you. She will be your companion."

"Oh, I hadn't thought about that." She'd been traveling through her corner of the world since childhood. The need for a chaperone had never come up.

He said nothing but offered a hand to assist her descent.

~

Rumpelstiltskin chose a seat at a table outside the tavern. Olsome strode to join him. Rom's lips twitched as his friend tugged on the leather jerkin he'd had to put on. "You look like a real soldier of this land."

Olsome rolled his eyes. "I'd much rather be home planting fields." He sat across the table from Rom. "How goes the mission?"

Rom shrugged. "Still waiting to see where this adventure leads us."

Another carriage, more opulent than any they had yet seen, rolled to a stop within the gravel yard of the tavern. They both watched a well-dressed servant open the door. At first, Rom thought it was a child who climbed down, but when he saw her face, he realized she was an adult.

The diminutive young woman surprised him. Her gown was wrinkled from traveling and half of her dark hair fell out of its knot. Rom considered for a moment to make an opportunity to greet her, but then thoughts of his purpose pulled his attention away. Perhaps later, if God saw fit, their paths could cross again.

Olsome glanced at him, one of his eyebrows raised. "We do not often meet someone of your height." He paused. "A very pretty someone."

Rom watched the woman follow her servant into the tavern. He shook his head. "Tempting though she may be our purpose is not my own."

"Perhaps there will be a better time."

"By God's will."

~

The next morning, a maid sat across from Elizabeth as the journey continued. The woman had a knitting project on her lap and another spilling from the carpet bag on the seat beside her. Other than a simple good morning and an offer to help however she might, she seemed disinclined to converse. Elizabeth held her book in her hand and stared out the window.

They should reach the palace today. The clouds in the sky weren't the sort to bring rain. She must have dozed because the carriage stopping caused her to straighten in her seat. They were somewhere that did not resemble the open spaces she was used to. Through the window she saw a wall of dark rock.

"You missed the vista of the palace from afar," the maid said as she wrapped her projects to return to the carpet bag. "Not that it would help you find your way around." She shivered. "I am glad I do not have to stay here with you."

"Will you take the carriage back?"

"Heavens, no. I'll catch the post in the village."

The door opened and the servant arranged the steps for them. He nodded at the maid. "Your assistance has been appreciated." He handed her an envelope. Then he helped Elizabeth from the carriage.

Moments later, strangers surrounded her. Elizabeth stood to the side of a stone entrance to… she wasn't sure where. Her trunk sat beside her. People gave her a look, as though it wasn't a place to be waiting with her luggage. The young servant had disappeared, though he promised to return for her. She looked up at the stone exterior and shivered. It wasn't just the crowds that made her long for home. Something about the place pressed on her. She frowned. What had Caro gotten herself into?

~

"What do you mean you are getting married? You have been here less than a fortnight." Elizabeth sank to the bed, unable to stand. Caroline had demanded she come to the palace, but she did not look in need of help. Her sister grinned with a sly smile. Elizabeth did not care for the change she could see. Caroline stood with her head high, ignoring the servants setting up the guestroom and building a fire in the fireplace. She knocked over the coal pail as she swept to Elizabeth's side.

"Caroline," Elizabeth admonished as she tried to help the young servant. Caroline dragged her away, pulling her to the window.

"It's happening, Lizzie. I have succeeded where many fail."

"How? It doesn't make sense. Where is Father?"

"Hunting with the princes. He wants this as much as I do. King Hewel made up his mind quickly, as did I."

Elizabeth moved closer, quieting her voice. "They say he can be cruel."

Caroline offered a knowing look. "I will give him no cause to be." She gave the room a glance and smiled. "You will be comfortable, Lizzie. I will see you at dinner. Wear something colorful if you have it. I will send my seamstress, Christina, to you in the morning."

Elizabeth watched her sister exit the room. She bit her nail as worry flustered her stomach. In the letter, Caro longed for her company, yet now she raced away before Elizabeth was even settled in her chamber. What changed in the days that had passed?

~

Hours later, Elizabeth stared at the solid door that had just been slammed in her face, and then turned to face her sister. "What is going on?"

"It was supposed to be over." Caroline wailed.

"What was supposed to be over? And why is there a mound of plants in a bedroom?"

Caroline sobbed harder. She grabbed Lizzie's arm. "Help me! Please, you must."

Elizabeth felt her heart melt at her sister's despairing look. All was not well, as she'd feared.

She shrugged her shoulders, confused. "Of course, I will help, but what is to be done? I do not understand."

"A pair of lovely ladies. I must have done something extraordinary to be blessed thusly. I am honored."

Elizabeth whirled around at the sound of a third person in the room. Near the door, although she would swear it had not opened, appeared a slender man. He stood much closer to her own diminutive height. High boots and buff pantaloons set off his navy jacket worn open at the front. He had a shock of red hair, and she could see freckles across his nose and cheeks. His eyes twinkled with laughter, and Elizabeth longed to laugh with him. She blinked, but he remained.

"This is…," Caroline frowned and waved her hand at him and then looked at her sister. "You said you would help. Help him. The king will spare us if the task is completed before dawn."

Elizabeth didn't understand the feelings rumbling through her heart. The man stepped closer. She could see flecks of green in his brown eyes.

"Elizabeth," Caroline jerked her around to face her. "Help him."

She shook her head, trying to clear it. "Help him do what?"

He walked around them and picked up a leaf of flax. "Turn this into gold."

She laughed, looking from the stranger to her sister and back again. Neither countenance changed, and her laughter faded into a nervous cough. "You are serious? But how is such a thing…"

He held his hand toward her as Caroline kissed her cheek. Her sister flopped onto the bed and turned away from them. Elizabeth could feel her forehead wrinkle as she returned her attention to the man. The hand he held to her had three fingers wrapped in cloths while the fourth boasted a nasty blister.

"Your fingers." Elizabeth gently took his hand and turned it palm up. She unwrapped one of the bandages and gasped at the red, weepy wound.

He tried to pull away, but she held tight. She gave him a hard glare. "Whatever you have been doing has not been good for you."

"It has been in service to another."

Elizabeth looked at the bed. "Caroline?"

He nodded.

Elizabeth shook her head. "I knew… I have something that may help." She pulled a small vial of salve from her handbag. "Works on dancing blisters, so it should help your wounds." Elizabeth led him to the chair beside the wheel. She knelt at his side and unwrapped each finger. Her lips tightened, but she tended his wounds as gently as she could.

She returned the vial to her bag and looked at the plants. "The flax did that?"

"Yes."

"Somehow you are able to turn it into gold? How is it even possible?"

"A gift."

"To be used by selfish people?" She glanced at her sister and then the locked door. "Why would you allow it to be this way?"

"Your sister's life was threatened."

"But now she sleeps."

34

"You may join her. I am able to complete the task on my own."

Her thoughts were not of sleep, nor of her sister. She stared at his eyes, drawn to their vibrant life. "I prefer helping you."

"Why?" His hoarse voice revealed he was as affected by her as she by him.

Their eyes held for a moment before he straightened, clearing his throat.

"We should begin if we want to complete the task by morning."

Elizabeth kept the pile of flax full as the stranger wove piece after piece into the ruts of the wheel. His feet turned the machine and in the blur of motion, bobbins filled with thread.

"Is this real gold?" Elizabeth placed another spool in the growing stack on the far wall.

"You must remember that with faith, nothing is impossible."

Elizabeth grunted. "A pity it goes to such a vile man."

"Gold will not change him. He will always hunger for more."

"As will Caroline?" She met his bright eyes over the whirl of the machine.

He agreed. Elizabeth felt sadness tug at her. "Why do you stay?"

"I cannot reveal that as yet." His lips twitched as his face brightened.

Her heart leapt at the sparkle in his eyes. She tugged at a wayward lock of her honey-colored hair and looked around. The pile of flax was gone. "That is all? The task is complete?" She reached for his hand. "What of your fingers? How did they fare?"

He managed to twist his hands, holding hers instead. Elizabeth felt him standing close to her, but she could not look up.

"Much better. A burden shared is a burden lifted." His breath fanned across her hairline.

"Caroline never helped?" Elizabeth wondered at the sound of her voice. He seemed to understand her, for he backed away a step, releasing her hands.

"She never thought to help. She's not cruel, just selfish."

Elizabeth could not refute his claim. She sighed.

"Take your rest. Morning will be here soon enough."

"Where will you sleep?" She found the courage to look at him. Already, his warm smile and dazzling eyes had worked their way into her heart.

A smile danced across his lips like a secret. "My bed is far from this place."

"You can leave, can't you? Without permission, just as you came?"

He pressed a finger to his lips. "Another secret I cannot share."

"Will I see you again?" She surprised herself by asking.

He held her hand once more. "Most definitely, if I please you."

Elizabeth nodded, unsure what to make of the stranger. A yawn grabbed her body.

With a laugh, he pushed her nearer her sister. "To bed."

~

The workings of God, the High King, should not

surprise him. Rom stared at the bed. She was the reason he had been selected for this particular task. He wiggled his fingers. The salve she'd used cut through the soreness. He rubbed his chin, wishing he still had the goatee. How would things work out? Excitement stirred. He couldn't wait to find out.

~

Elizabeth was surprised she slept and woke feeling rested. There were no windows in the room, so she couldn't tell if dawn had come. A low fire in the fireplace provided enough light to see. Caroline still slept. Elizabeth thinned her lips as she stared at the spools stacked against the wall. There had to be hundreds of them. From the opulence she'd witnessed throughout the palace, why did the king need so much gold? An impossible question.

"Is it morning already?" Caroline asked as she stretched.

Elizabeth turned, hands on her hips. "How can I tell. How many times has the king done this to you? What on earth would make him believe you could weave flax into gold?"

Caroline fixed her hair as she sat on the edge of the bed. "Father said something on one of his trips."

"What would have happened if that man didn't appear? Do you even know his name?"

Caroline waved. "It's probably a secret. Does it matter? I'll be married and we'll never see him again."

"What if King Hewel decides he wants more gold?" Elizabeth asked, stepping closer.

Caroline dropped her hands on her lap and frowned. "He wouldn't do that, or maybe our strange little friend will always appear to help."

Elizabeth heard the lock and then the door opened. Caroline jumped to her feet. Any concern she'd been feeling faded from her face. She glided to the man standing there. Elizabeth crossed her arms and watched as Caroline cooed.

"King Hewel. Aaden."

The king reached for her hand. "I am pleased you have succeeded in this challenge yet again." He kissed her cheek. "I have arranged for your things to be moved to a more fitting suite of rooms. Preparations for our wedding will begin."

"I look forward to it." She gazed at him with adoration.

Elizabeth rolled her eyes.

The king either didn't see or chose to ignore her. "Would you like your sister to move with you?"

"Oh, no." Caroline placed her hand on his arm as she peered at her sister. "I fear my little sister is not used to so many people. Moving her deeper into the palace would be unpleasant for her."

He looked at her with concern. "There will be a ball to announce our engagement in a week's time. Will she attend?"

Caroline smiled. "If she has not begged me to send her home, I shall insist."

The two of them walked away, arm in arm.

Chapter 5

Caroline wanted to enjoy the amenities of her new rooms, but Lizzie's comments harped within her mind. She paced. What if the king needed more gold one day? It might not matter if she were his queen, or he could use it as an opportunity to be rid of her.

The little man had magical powers, but perhaps, there was a way to hold onto him. The dungeon was not a nice place, but she could make a space as comfortable as possible. But how could she capture him? He came and went in the room as he pleased, but was there a way to counter that ability? Who would know enough to help her?

She paused at a window. "Mrs. Joust." The old woman ran the herbalist shop in the village. Her knowledge went to more than herbs and medicines. She would have an idea. The thought brought hope. Caroline settled into her bed. She could claim she needed to go shopping for the ball. She had her plan for the morning.

~

"Names are very important," Mrs. Joust twisted a lid onto a bottle as she considered Caroline's dilemma. "What was his name?"

"He never said."

Mrs. Joust snapped her finger. "Of course, that has to be the secret. There are plenty of legends where having someone's name gives one control over that person."

"How do I find out his name?"

"Can't ask him. No reason to trust he'd tell you the truth anyway. Is there anyone else who's seen him?"

"My sister, Elizabeth."

"Did he treat her any differently than you?"

Caroline shrugged. "She helped him."

"Maybe he told her. Or you could ask her to find out for you."

"Oh, no. She would not approve of my plan."

Mrs. Joust was silent for a moment, and then her face brightened with a smile. "Accuse him of something horrific. Make her think he deserves whatever happens to him."

Caroline tapped her chin. "Bad enough he insisted on my sister as payment." She pressed a hand against her chest. "I had already given him what money and jewels I had." Her eyes brightened. "I could claim he has demanded my firstborn child as payment. Elizabeth would never stand for such a thing."

Mrs. Joust shook her head. "That is quite a story. Are you certain you can tell it well enough?"

"My talent is weaving. I may not be able to make gold, but I can weave a story not even Lizzie can deny is true."

Excitement with the plan made Caroline want to

rush back to the palace, but she needed to gather supplies for the ball. Her sister would have nothing appropriate to wear. After saying farewell to Mrs. Joust, with a promise to return to tell her the outcome of all things, Caroline wandered further into the village. There wasn't time to have a dress made. She stopped at a clothier. She hadn't expected to find anything close to fitting Elizabeth's diminutive size, and yet, a silver gown caught her eye. Silver lame net covered a silver and white satin slip. The lines were simple with a tie beneath the chest and short sleeves edged with lace. It could have been made for a child. Still a bit long, but someone in the palace should be able to fit the hem correctly.

"I fear, I do not have the fabric to fit it to your size, my dear." A round woman with thick curly hair greeted her.

Caroline shook her head. "For my sister. She is quite small." She touched fabric that seemed to shimmer. "Have it delivered to the palace this afternoon."

"By who's authority?"

Caroline showed her the seal Chancellor Mornn had given her that morning.

The woman glowed. "My lady, of course. I shall deliver it myself."

~

Elizabeth stared out the window, longing to walk in the woods, not merely see them in the distance. "I should know better than to make promises with Caro. Where is that girl?" She muttered, but the window offered no answers.

Noise in the hallway drew her attention, and

then her door burst open, and Caroline entered. Three women followed her, one of whom carried a dress in her arms.

"What are you doing?" Elizabeth asked in way of greeting.

"I found the perfect dress for you. For the ball."

Elizabeth frowned. "I do not need a new gown."

Caroline gave her one of those looks. "You have nothing good enough for a king's ball. Besides, I think you will approve of this one."

Elizabeth didn't want to like anything, but the shimmering silver in a simple form charmed her. "It is beautiful," she gasped.

Caroline looked pleased. "I thought you would like it."

"It will need to be taken up," the older woman spoke. She motioned for the girls to take measurements of Elizabeth.

Task complete, they whisked the dress away. Caroline took her hands. "I am pleased you like the gown. I have other things to do. Have you seen father?"

Elizabeth shook her head.

"Well, I will be sure he joins us for dinner. Tonight, will be simple and quiet. Everyone is preparing for tomorrow's ball."

Elizabeth did not mind simple and quiet.

~

The following evening, Elizabeth stood in front of a long mirror as a maid laced the gown. "It's still a bit long." The fabric trailed the floor. She touched the skirt.

"You look beautiful. Like a fairy." The girl

sighed.

Elizabeth giggled. "I feel like a princess." But was it right? Though she'd been at the palace for days, she still felt uneasy. Caroline hoped the king would make an announcement. Why would she still desire to marry the man? The horrid things he'd required of her... Elizabeth shook her head.

"Is something wrong?" the maid asked with a nervous search.

"Oh no, this is perfect." Elizabeth turned around. "I'm not used to the grand scale of the palace. I'd much rather attend a small gathering at home."

The maid patted her arm. "This is a grand place, but you never know, you may find the one treasure of value amongst all the noise."

The words stayed with her, even much later in the evening when the press of people in the ballroom grew thick. Someone's elbow almost knocked her in the head. She'd arrived with Caroline and her father, but both had disappeared. Elizabeth ducked around a potted plant and sought a door into a quiet room. But she found herself outside instead. She could still hear the musicians, but this terrace had no lights. No people. She breathed in the quiet, smiling at the scent of jasmine in the air.

~

Rom flexed his fingers after removing the wraps. The salve Elizabeth used had them healing nicely. Thoughts of her brought a smile to his face. Tonight, was the ball. She would doubtless dance and find herself with a line of suiters. He sighed, even though the thought felt off. She would not find much

to appreciate in the press of a king's ball. He rubbed
his chin. Perhaps he should attend. Seek her out.

Chapter 6

M y lady, why do you hide in the dark?"

Elizabeth spun around with a gasp and then smiled at the man who joined her. "It's you."

He bowed with flourish, elegant sleeves falling from a velvety jacket of deep green. The fitted pants, delicate knot at his neck, and black leather shoes complimented his physique and Elizabeth felt herself fumble for confidence. The evening gown her sister had provided swept across the ground and she feared tripping at every step.

"An odd place to stand when attending a ball." He placed his hands in his pockets and leaned against a stone wall.

She grimaced. Beyond the open door, a cacophony of color milled throughout the opulent ballroom.

"A dainty such as yourself probably gets lost among so many." He nodded at the crowds they could see through open arches leading into the ballroom.

"I've been mistaken for a child more than once." Her sigh encapsulated frustration and embarrassment. "I admit, my pleasure is wandering in the gardens."

"But since we are here." He took a step closer, holding one hand to her.

She glanced at the doorway.

"We can dance on the terrace, if you like. Do you hear the music?"

Elizabeth placed her hand in his. "I do." Her forehead wrinkled. "I do not even know your name. I never thought to ask it of you the other night."

He bowed and kissed her hand. His warm lips sent shivers up her arm. "Rumpelstiltskin. Yes, I know. A mouthful."

She watched him smile as she tried repeating his name.

"Friends call me Rom. Come, they have started a waltz."

Laughter bubbled within her as he twirled her, one hand at her waist, the other firmly holding her hand. She enjoyed the movement of muscle beneath his shoulder where her other hand held him. Music seemed to swell around them as they stepped together across the empty terrace. Worry about her skirts faded as her senses filled with him.

"Ah, my dear Elizabeth," he whispered against her ear as they stilled. "I knew God sent me for a reason. It is you. I am here because of you."

Her hand lay against his chest, and she could feel his heart beating. Beating for her. "How is it even possible?"

He didn't answer with words. He kissed her. She fit perfectly against him. Never had she known such emotion. Her arms wrapped around him. Time halted, hovered above them, as they stood together beneath the full moon.

"Oh, my." She sighed as they parted.

"Lizzie," he spoke her name with laughter and joy.

She lay her head against his chest. His arms wrapped around her, and she could feel his cheek against the top of her head as his hand caressed her hair.

"Lizzie, Lizzie."

The sound of her name spoken with his accent sent shivers down her spine.

He continued. "Your sister will be queen. They will expect you to make a match with a count or a baron."

Backing away, she studied his face. A lock of wavy hair fluttered across his forehead. She knew in her heart she would find nothing better inside the ballroom. "I am content to remain here with you."

"Walk with me." He tucked her arm in his elbow. Steps leading from the terrace to the gardens were lit. More lights bobbled throughout the palace garden as a slight breeze fluttered the trees.

"Where is your home, Rom?" What could she learn about this man at her side?

"Beyond the mountain pass to the north."

"I have never travelled to the mountains."

"Summer is the best season. The alpine fields bloom with wildflowers. The air is as sweet as honey and butterflies dance upon the wind." He picked a dandelion that had gone to seed. With a light breath, feathery puffs floated around them.

She laughed. "Do forests not cover the

mountains?"

"Not in the highest reaches."

His hand brushed hers, and she intertwined her fingers with his. "When do you return home?"

"When my purpose here is met."

"The king's gold?" She grimaced. "That is your purpose?"

The scent of lilacs curled around them. Rom reached for a bloom and placed it in her other hand.

"I came because of a request to protect. At first, it did not make sense. But now it has been made clear. I will return home when my heart's desire goes with me. For now, let us enjoy the garden, and perhaps another dance?"

Elizabeth tucked the bloom in a pocket and offered her hand to him. She fell in love twirling to the harmony of crickets and mating frogs. As the moon began to descend to the west, they returned to the castle and paused beside an empty door standing open. The ballroom sounded far away. Elizabeth rubbed a braided cord that lined his jacket. He lifted her hand and placed a gentle kiss in her palm. She hoped the joy in his face was mirrored in her own.

"I do not know when next we will meet," he said.

"Will you attend the wedding?"

"You may have need of me before then. Woods lay to the east, call for me there."

"The woods?"

He must have noticed her puzzled glance, for he laughed. "Trust me. If I do not come for you myself, look for me there."

Smiling, she shook her head. "Mystery upon

mystery, but I will find you."

He lifted his hands to her face, drawing her close until their lips touched. His sweet kiss made her head swirl. He pulled away but remained close enough for his breath to stir tendrils of hair drooping at her temples. "I will leave you now, dear Lizzie. Dream of me."

She did just that.

Chapter 7

It is the most horrid nightmare! Elizabeth, what am I to do?"

Elizabeth jumped, started from her daydream. Caroline raced across the library, to her side. Falling to her knees, she took Elizabeth's hands.

"We are done for. That horrid man." Tears poured from Caroline's red-rimmed eyes.

Elizabeth's heart twisted with fear. "What has the king done?"

"Isn't the king." Her sister sobbed, drawing shallow breaths. "It's him. That one who helped us." She released Elizabeth and scraped at tears pouring down her cheeks. "I offered compensation. He never said a word, so I assumed it would be enough. But he wants more."

Elizabeth pulled away with an exasperated sigh. "This has nothing to do with gold, Caro, he wants me…"

Caroline shook her head. "No, Elizabeth. He has demanded our first child. I must swear to it."

"What do you mean, first child?"

Caroline blushed and turned her head. "When

the king and I… after we're married."

Elizabeth frowned. "No. Rom isn't like that."

Caroline's attention perked up. "Rom?"

"Rumpelstiltskin. But he isn't like that. He cares about me."

Caroline shook her head fiercely. "He doesn't care if you live or die." She grabbed Lizzie's hands again, squeezing painfully. "Neither of us. Without a promise, he will take the gold and the king will put us to death."

Elizabeth pulled her hands from her sister's grip. Something akin to anger began to simmer within her. "I don't believe you. I know him."

"Know him?" Caroline's voice lashed as she leapt to her feet. "How can you know him? I have seen more of him than you. He is a trickster and a liar."

"I don't believe you."

"Then let us meet with him together." Caroline looked down her nose. "Let him speak truth to us both. We will know who the liar is."

~

Elizabeth slammed the guest room door, having left Caroline in the library. How dare she speak thus? Blood had stained the fabric wrapped around Rom's fingers. Tricksters and liars didn't harm themselves in saving others. She paused in front of a gilded mirror. "But if not him, Caroline is the liar." Could she believe it of her sister? She nodded, though her chest clenched. She faced the window where a box garden and green field gave way to trees in the distance.

Elizabeth ran through the garden to a path

leading into a wild, wooded area. "Rom?" she shouted into the bands of trees. He appeared from the shadows before she called a second time.

"Elizabeth. What has happened?"

She ran to him, wrapping her arms around his waist. His strength seeped through the cold as he held her. There was no need to even ask. She could sense he was honest and true. She snuggled closer with a sigh of contentment.

He murmured an endearment and kissed the top of her head. And then he tensed.

Elizabeth turned as her sister rustled into the open. She stepped out of his embrace. "Caroline? What are you doing here?" Elizabeth did not give her time to answer. "You lied, didn't you? But why--?"

Caroline's face hardened. She ignored Elizabeth and focused on Rom. "I realized that even once I am queen, I may have need of your particular skill. What if the king requires more gold? I need you to stay."

Rom pulled Elizabeth behind him, and she watched him face her sister. "This is not my home."

"No, it isn't." Caroline stepped closer. "But it will be your prison."

He laughed. "You have no power to keep such a one as me."

"I do if I know your name."

"Caroline, stop this." Elizabeth lunged forward.

"Rumpelstiltskin." Caroline spoke his name as a curse.

Elizabeth cried out as Rom fell to his knees with a shout of pain. "No!" She tried to touch him, but he pushed her away. His eyes darkened, and she felt lost.

"What is this?" She turned her accusation to her sister. "I do not understand."

"His name, dear sister." Caroline's smile chilled. She stroked his cheek. Elizabeth watched him strain, as though bound with heavy rope. "He is one whose name is precious. He came because the Great one called his name. He will remain because of me."

Elizabeth pushed her away. "You cannot do this. You must not! Release him."

"So I can die? You care that little for your own flesh and blood?"

"Your lies have brought you here. Rom has done nothing but try to help us."

"And he will continue to help me." Caroline motioned, and a pair of soldiers stepped forward. "Lock him away." She ordered.

Elizabeth watched, helpless, as they dragged Rom through the trees. He wouldn't even look at her. Fear pounded her heart, so recently light with love. She ran after them, determined to find a way to help.

Caroline snatched her arm, and Elizabeth yelped as sharp nails raked her skin. "Be careful. I can find another cell your size."

"Do not do this, Caroline. He is a good man. He doesn't deserve such treatment."

"What do you think the king will do with you, little sister?"

"Does it matter?" Elizabeth wrenched herself from her sister's grip. "I will not be like you, with your cold heart. Since when does gold matter more than life?"

"You don't understand."

"I don't want to." She ran after the guards and Rumpelstiltskin.

LAURIE LEE

Chapter 8

D eath clung to the air like icicles in the rafters. The king's dungeon was dim and cold. Its walls dripped with misery. Elizabeth saw the same guards turn a corner devoid of their prisoner. They paid her no heed as they quickened their pace toward their midday meal. She peeked around the edge of the wall. A lone door stood at the end of a short hallway. She ran, falling to her knees beside it.

"Rom," she called through the thick door. "Forgive me, I did not know. Please, my love. Forgive me!"

Something shuffled, and hope flared briefly. But silence reined.

"I am here. I will not leave you. We will find a way to break my sister's hold." Elizabeth sobbed, curling against the door. Shivers brought goose bumps to her arms, but she kept one hand pressed against the wood of the door. "I am here, my love."

She must have slept, for a strange howl startled her. She looked around. A single torch continued to provide light. She rested her head against the door with a sigh and pounded her hand against it.

"I am here with you, Rom." The dungeon

remained eerily quiet. Tears pooled in her eyes, and she prayed for help.

"Sleeping in damp dungeons is not good for your health. You are supposed to be in your room."

Elizabeth cried out, and then her eyes widened as Rom knelt beside her. He wrapped a wool blanket over her shoulders. Confused, she looked at the locked door, and then at him. Her mouth hung open for a moment as she tried to determine if she slept.

He swept her up in his arms, carrying her with one hand behind her back and the other beneath her knees. She threw an arm around his shoulder. Dream or not, she found herself where she wanted to be. She nestled more comfortably against his chest and tried to stop a sob.

"Do not cry, dear Elizabeth." He nuzzled her neck, causing a shiver. "Your sister does not understand the nature of my people. I was led here by God."

She could feel his body shake and it took a moment to realize he laughed.

"Why would she suppose using my name would keep me here?"

"But you were in pain, so angry with me."

"A bit of dramatic flair." He had the grace to give her a sheepish look. "I'm afraid your sister's heart has turned to stone. I had to let her think she could capture me."

"Why are you still here? You should have escaped by now."

"I will not leave without you, my dear. You are my heart's desire."

"You might have gotten away if you had." The

king's strong voice bounced against the stone walls of the hallway. He blocked their path, holding a long, thin sword pointed at them.

Rom set Elizabeth on her feet and pushed her behind him.

"Where is my gold?" King Hewel snarled, each word chilling.

Rom clicked his tongue. "You have grown too greedy, Sire."

"It is necessary for a king. The spools are gone. Where did you hide them?"

"Plants wither and die. That is what has happened to your gold spun from flax. Did you really suppose you could bend the nature of one thing into another?"

"Caroline says you have claimed her power. You stole the gold for your own purpose."

"What honor is there in a king who would attack an unarmed man?"

King Hewel's eyes traveled from head to foot as a sneer curled his lip. Elizabeth gripped Rom's sleeve.

"Am I to fear you, little man?"

"Give me a sword and we will see. If I lose, I restore your gold."

"If you lose? There is no if, boy. You'll be dead." He pointed his sword at Elizabeth. "Be sure she knows your secrets. I'll enjoy beating them out of her."

Elizabeth stiffened. "You'll not lay a hand on me, vile man."

The king's laughter echoed through the dungeon. "To the soldiers' field." He snagged

Elizabeth, twisting his hand through her hair. She cried out, and stumbled as the king forced her forward. She didn't have to see Rom to know he followed. Fear eased, though the pain of her scalp caused tears in her eyes.

The soldiers' field spread like a green carpet over a slight hill. Early morning light bathed the area in its golden glow. Elizabeth remained on the ground where the king had pushed her. Clutching the blanket with trembling fingers, she watched Chancellor Mornn offer a rapier to Rom. "Please, Lord. Protect him. Let evil be defeated," she prayed as Rom and the king circled. Others hovered as well, but her focus remained on the battle.

Blades cracked against one another. King Hewel lunged forward. Rom skipped aside, his smaller stature providing quick bursts of movement. He eluded the king. Elizabeth watched the larger man roar with frustration. Metal against metal, over and over, until she covered her eyes. But the feel of the battle rumbled through the ground on which she sat. She peeked through her fingers, and then gasped as Rom went down. He rolled quickly and flew to his feet once more. His fluid motion added to the king's anger. His motions grew wild. One hand slipped behind his back. Something gleamed in the increasing light.

Elizabeth jumped to her feet. "Watch out, he has a dagger!"

Rom twisted as the king lunged. Elizabeth watched in horror as a line of blood appeared across Rom's upper arm. The smaller man danced aside. The king overstepped his bound and fell forward. He lay in the grass, face-down. Sunlight burst through the clouds and lit the field. Elizabeth stared, barely breathing. Rom's sword dropped to the ground. He knelt beside the fallen king. His head bow for a moment before he reached across and rolled him over.

She took a step closer. "Is he…"

Rom placed his hand on the King's neck. "He lives."

A guard knocked Rom away. "Get a flat."

Elizabeth sprinted to Rom. His good arm wrapped around her shoulders as they watched men lifted the king onto a board.

"What have you done? Is he dead?" Caroline's enraged scream flew across the field. To Elizabeth's surprise, she rushed past them and fell at the king's side.

"You should take your leave while their attention is elsewhere."

Elizabeth saw another soldier stand beside Rom. He handed him a leather satchel. "Here, my Lord. Two horses await outside the gate. Use the lower entrance. It is open and unguarded."

They shook hands. "Be well, Olsome." Rom slapped his arm. "Be swift in getting yourself removed from this place."

With a final glance of Caroline bending over the king, Elizabeth allowed Rom to lead her from the soldier's field. His fast pace quickened her breath, but her mind puzzled the words she'd heard.

"Why did he call you my Lord?" Elizabeth asked.

"Did I not mention I am a king's son?"

"A king's…?" she stumbled, but he kept her moving forward. "But he would have killed you."

"Even death would be worth it, having met you."

"But I could not bear it."

They came to an arched opening and paused. He pulled her close. "I am thankful God pulled us through."

She looked up at him and his hand caressed her cheek. Love shone from his eyes.

"Ride home with me." His voice drew her closer. "Be my bride. We shall send word to your father once you are safe."

Joy rose through her, filling the dark, lonesome, fearful corners within her. Her answer must have shone in her eyes, because he kissed her. A short kiss filled with promise and a future together.

They rode toward the mountains.

The Pied Piper
(fairytale of the same name)

The tale of the pied piper may very well be based on real events as far in the past as the 13th century. An inscription on a house in Hamelin, Germany sets the date as 26 June. One-hundred-thirty children disappeared. They were last seen following a colorful piper into the hills. The Brothers Grimm wrote the story down in their 1816 German Legends collection of tales.

This retelling still involves peril to children. Be warned, if that is of concern to you. Otherwise, enjoy reading.

LAURIE LEE

Wyrwhith Tavern bustled with customers as sunlight burst through the relentless cloud bank that had daunted travelers for a day and a half. A toddler wailed as a pair of siblings chased each other between tables.

"Watch your goings." A large man growled as the taller child knocked the table and beer splashed across worn wood. The boy offered a saucy grin before returning to the chase. Dale swiped a hand across his mouth, hiding the smile he was unable to prevent.

"I don't want to sit." A girl toward the front of the room yelled. She swiped her hand across the table to strike her mother.

Her father's hand connected with her cheek. "You'll not talk to your mother that way."

Dale could feel the buzz of unspent energy circling the room. Most were going on too little sleep. The accommodations couldn't hold all the people, so they'd spent the night curled up in corners or beneath tables.

Beams of light shone through the windows. The rain had ceased, but it would take time to clear the roads and prepare to resume travel. The children needed something now to draw their attention.

Music pulsed through his body. He lifted the worn tapestry carpetbag nestled on the stool beside him to his lap. Pushing the change of clothes aside, his fingers brushed against the flute. The wood instrument caused his fingers to tingle. Excitement built inside him. He grabbed a bar towel and tipped a bottle of oil. He rubbed the oil along the flute. His gaze wandered through the tavern's common room as he lifted the instrument to his lips.

With a deep breath, he blew through the end. Moving one finger to the first hole, the musical note rose. The cacophony of noise in the room dimmed. He placed a second finger and the tone rose even higher. He watched the room. The siblings who had been chasing one another froze in their steps and turned to watch him. The crying toddler silenced. All eyes turned to him. Dale stood and played a short melody, a series of notes that wound up and down, like a line of children skipping through the room. He continued to play as he stepped around the table. His fingers moved across the holes of the flute. A few children followed, their faces lit with wonder and fun. Parents offered tired smiles as the line of children increased. He moved to and fro among the tables. Light outside the main door beckoned. Music surrounded him. He danced through the doors. Mud splashed his shoes, but he didn't care.

Dale played through the streets, winding his way along alleys and across short rock fences. He played, and all around him children danced. They twirled. They sang. They ran in circles with joined hands. The music played on.

~

A rumble of voices drew Dale from slumber. He winced at the feel of hard earth beneath him. Where was he? He searched his memories, but the images were as hazy as a faint dusting of fog. He stretched and opened his eyes. Through the veil of green, he saw a baton swinging toward him. He swerved out of the way, but the wooden tool struck his shoulder. He rolled, howling with anger and pain. Half a dozen men reached for him.

"Hold!" He screamed out, snatching the baton as it swung again at his head.

He shook his head, trying to staunch the haze of pain and sleep. They were muttering and yelling incoherently. He heard the words 'children' and 'lost'.

"What has happened?" He tried to stand, but a large farmer knocked him down.

"Let him be." A woman's voice broke through the commotion.

Dale watched, amazed, as the disgruntled villagers lowered their arms. A figure draped in black approached.

"Where are they? What has he done with them?" The cries of the men gathered to attack him tore at his heart. He could hear desperation and despondency in their voices. What had happened?

The stranger lowered her cowl. Gleaming hair the color of moonlight streamed from her head. He could not see her face, but something about the hair tickled his memory.

"The children are not here. You have naught but speculation against him. Leave be. I will help as I may to recover those who have been lost." Her strong voice carried into the woods.

The group dispersed, seeming to fade into the waning shadows.

Dale breathed deeply to calm his racing heart. "How did you convince them to leave?" He pressed his hand against his injured shoulder. "I thought they meant to kill me." Dale struggled to his feet and then froze as the woman turned her face to him. Her features were of one that haunted his dreams. His nightmares. He drew a lock of her hair from beneath her cape, allowing it to drift through his fingers. "I remember you." Memories crashed into his awareness.

~

On a day when the sun shone in a blue sky and the air felt warm with summer's breath, two children raced along the bank of a river keeping eyes on a boat made from burnt wood and a bit of cloth. Dale looked from the feisty girl in front of him to the ship they had built.

"Run! We'll never catch our sail," she cried back to him, her voice a mixture of giggles and determination. Dale laughed as he increased his speed. The river was stealing their sailboat. He dodged tree roots and hurtled across crags as he chased after the vivid red ponytail of his best friend. They followed the river as far as they could, but the sailboat, freshly carved and hoisted, sped further and further from their reach. The growing tangle of brambles blocked their path and they had to turn aside.

Dale leaned his hands on his knees, breathing hard and laughing uncontrollably. She doubled over, her own laughter filling the woods.

Morgan. That was her name.

A bird perched on a tree nearby and squawked

its displeasure at their disturbance. The odd creature gleamed in the afternoon sunlight streaming amongst the trees. Various shades of blue sparkled in its feathers.

"Have you seen anything like it?" Morgan took a step closer. The bird remained on its perch, beady eyes glaring at them both.

"From where do you suppose it is come?" Dale asked breathlessly.

Neither gave a thought to the sailboat, their full attention turning to the unusual bird. It fluttered a few trees away and turned back, gazing at them once more. The pair of children exchanged a look, and then gave chase.

The bird led them further and further from the river, deeper and deeper into the forest where trees stood closer together. Light dimmed and the branches around them grew gnarled and twisted. The bird kept them to a path they could traverse, until they broke through the brambles and entered a clearing.

The bird disappeared. Dale gaped as Morgan grabbed his hand. Clear blue sky shone above them, and a strange house stood on the far side of the clearing. Its windowpanes were bright blue. The hemispheres above the windows were purple. The walls were white. Its steep pitch roof overhung the walls and curved outward.

The bird had been enchanting, but this... He stepped closer, desiring to touch the rich colors they beheld. Morgan stayed at his side, her hand tightening on his. The wood door opened, and a woman stepped onto the porch, stilting their progress. Though her skin looked smooth, and her hair was the color of oak, something about her gave the impression of great age.

"My, my, my. What have we here? Have you come to visit old Meg?" She put one foot onto the upper step of her porch. And then the other one. "Meg's a lonely woman. She don't get to visit often." She moved to the next step.

"We're sorry. We didn't realize anyone lived here." Morgan found her voice first.

"Don't be sorry, child. How else am I to meet people, then if they come unawares?"

"You live here by yourself?" Dale asked.

Meg smiled. "As alone as one can be in the woods." She stepped to the ground and walked closer to the children. "What lovely hair you have child. That color is..."

The few moments of silence caused the hairs on his neck to bristle.

"Brilliant." The old woman continued. "Red as the autumn apple harvest." She moved closer. "And your eyes. Cerulean blue. I've not seen the like."

Dale shivered. The woman's attention seemed completely fixed on Morgan, yet he couldn't move. He wanted to. He wanted to pull Morgan back and run through the twisted and garbled trees until they found the river once more. He wanted to get away from the stranger named Meg. But he couldn't move. He could only watch as she moved closer and closer to Morgan.

"I had daughters once. Long ago, but they were never so sweet. Not a one bore colors as vivid as you."

He watched Morgan flinch as Meg reached for her hair. They should run, but neither seemed capable of going anywhere. Meg didn't just touch the silken red strands of Morgan's hair. She curled it around her hand and pulled.

Morgan began to scream as though she were in pain. He snatched at Meg's hand, but the old woman knocked him to the ground.

Her dark look held him to the ground. "Your turn comes soon enough, boy."

Before his eyes, Morgan's hair began to streak with white. She fell to her knees, struggling still. Dale curled his fingers into the dirt as he watched the bland door turn a brilliant shade of red. A streak of blue washed across a white wall. Finally, Morgan lay in the dirt as the witch panted with excitement. Morgan's hair had turned silvery white. She looked at him, and he could see her face had been bleached of color as well. She staggered back on her hands and knees as Meg released her. She looked as though she had been drained into a pale semblance of a girl.

The witch turned her attention to Dale. He saw Morgan stagger to her feet and run away. He reached for her, but she turned her back. The last he saw was the streak of her white hair disappearing into the shadow of the trees.

~

Morgan snatched her hand from his and drew her cloak around herself. She stared. He gulped. Her eyes were the same pale gray color he'd seen staring at him in the clearing so many years ago. He could see recognition in them.

"I left you," Morgan whispered.

Dale couldn't seem to find his words. He could only stare. Those memories, they had no place in his mind.

Morgan reached for him, but dropped her hand before her fingers touched his skin. "I thought she killed you." Her voice sounded full of wonder and pain. "You never returned. Your parents couldn't bear living in the village. They left." Her eyes filled with tears. "I never spoke... I didn't know how to explain."

Dale shook his head. "You're not a real memory." He backed away, his brows furrowing as he fought the onslaught of images that overlapped. "Your hair was red, like the door. I hated that door. I tried to paint over it once, but the red bled through. It wouldn't go away."

"You stayed there?" Morgan drew her cape close as she stared. "What did she do to you, Dale?"

"No." He put his hand up to stop her from stepping closer. "Mother lives in the woods. That's where I grew up. I've lived there my whole life. Without father. He died long before I could remember him."

"But you know that's not true. You know me, don't you?"

"But how? I don't understand." He pressed his hands to his eyes, trying to block the sunlight. Pain sliced his head as memories warred with one another.

He felt Morgan's hands touch his, drawing them from his face. "Let's not think on the past for now. Focus here. When did you arrive in the village?"

"Yesterday, midmorning. It was pouring rain and our coach pulled in to wait it out." He furrowed his brow, trying to think through the fog. "Or was it the day before?"

"The sun came out in the afternoon yesterday."

He nodded. "Then it was the day before. Yesterday, the children were restless. I started playing my flute to distract them."

"Your flute?"

"I'm a minstrel. The bar master paid me to play the night before. Yesterday I played for fun."

"The children were in the street. I heard them. I stood on the stoop and watched you lead them up the hill."

"But to help." His voice broke. "The children were tired of being locked inside because of the rain. I came back for my bag afterward." He kicked the carpet bag leaning against the tree. He'd used it as his pillow. "I don't know where the children went. I thought they went home."

But Morgan shook her head. "None of them returned down the hill. I heard the villagers. They waited. Your music faded, as though you led them further and further away."

"It doesn't make sense. I didn't do anything with the children. I would never hurt… I couldn't hurt them."

"It's the witch." Morgan's face became hard. "She did something to you. She has the children. We must find them."

Wordless questions caused the pain in his head to intensify, even as Morgan's touch calmed the anxious beating of his heart. He knew her, and that knowing threatened to topple his world. "We must seek the truth." A hoarse whisper was all he could manage.

~

"We wait until dark." Morgan sat on the ground a few feet from him. From Dale. He lived. Was it possible? She glanced toward him. With his head leaned against the tree, eyes closed, he looked older. Harder. Same blonde hair. Same blue eyes. She pulled on her hair that had been drained of color. Why her and not him? She swallowed. That wasn't fair. He lived, but at what cost? She closed her eyes. It would be a long day.

Hours later, Morgan tightened the cinch on her saddle as she took a quick glance at Dale preparing his mount. He didn't speak, just followed her directions like a child. She moved her horse to a log she could use to help mount the horse. She placed her foot in the stirrup and pulled herself up. Twilight settled over them as they moved to the village. Voices cried in the night.

"Stephanie," a woman called, but her voice cracked, as though she had been at it since dawn.

They road past another parent crouched in a doorway of the inn holding a stuffed toy. Morgan led the horses along a fence so they could pass without being seen. Within minutes, they were through the village following the road south.

"Am I responsible?" Dale's soft tone caused her to jump.

She could hear the catch in his voice. Despair. She gripped his hand. "We will find them. We'll make this right."

"Music is not an evil thing."

"No." Morgan turned her head at the shrill cry

of an animal hiding in the dark. Shivers ran along her back. She turned once more to Dale. "No. The evil lies with the witch."

"I don't see how she can be considered evil." He pressed the heel of his hands against his eyes as his horse followed Morgan. "Mother is a lovely woman."

"She is not your mother." Morgan felt her throat tighten with emotion. "I remember your mother crying. I had to listen to her, nothing to ease my feel of guilt. I left you back there, abandoned you, my dearest friend." Morgan rested her head against the horse as sobs shook her body. Years weighed on her shoulders, yet here was Dale riding beside her on the empty road. She felt a hand on her back, rubbing in circles.

"I am sorry." She could barely breathe. The horse was stopped, and she found herself in his arms. "I was scared. I didn't understand what had happened. I thought she meant to kill us. And I left you there to die."

"But I am not dead." The air of his words brushed against her hair. He held her for a time. It was strangely familiar and oh so unusual. Hardly anyone dared touch the paleness she'd become. Did any remember the deep red color of her hair? The blue of her eyes? Crowded thoughts drew her away from Dale.

She returned to her horse. Morgan wiped her eyes. Now was the time to look forward, not think back. What had happened to the children? Could they find them in time to save them? Night crawled. The sound of hooves against the road mesmerized her, but she fought against the pull of sleep. Further they must go.

It wasn't until the eastern horizon began to lighten that Morgan allowed them to stop. Dale seemed pensive, an obedient child once more. He laid a blanket for her and one for himself further away. Morgan curled beneath her cloak. Her mind whirled as light crept into the forest. She forced her eyes closed. *God, lead us well, for I am filled with fear*. She repeated the prayer until merciful sleep pulled her free.

~

She'd been dreaming. When she opened her eyes, she'd find herself at home in the back field. She wasn't steps away from Dale. She opened her eyes. Trees, late afternoon gloom, and the sight of Dale studying his flute greeted her.

"Good morning." He smiled as he closed his carpet bag.

"We have fewer hours to evening."

He laughed, throwing his head back and allowing a rich, resonate laughter to fill the air. Morgan couldn't stop her responding smile.

"Yes, so it is, Morgan-girl. We should be going."

He folded the blankets as she stretched and traveled a little way to take care of business.

When they were ready, she allowed him to take the lead. As the horses moved with an easy gate, Morgan studied the man. He would be close to twenty-five, a year older than herself. Wide shoulders, but would he be reliable? Straight back, but would he be honest? That her heart wanting to trust him confused her. He had been more than ten years in the control of a witch. The manner of man he had grown into could not be of quality. And yet, she saw her childhood friend in him. She sighed. The horse plodded on as her mind battled with emotions.

~

Dale slowed his horse as they approached a village. There wasn't supposed to be anything along this path.

"Where are we?" Morgan asked as she came abreast.

Dale gripped the horse's lead. "I haven't been here before." He hadn't. But if that were true, how could this be the path home? They dismounted to pass through the city gates. The strangeness of the town made his blood run cold. How could he not know villages that the road home passed through?

The horses' hooves clomped on the cobblestone street. Morgan stood with him, for which he was grateful. The gray, quiet village ate at his heart. Gray dominated the landscape. Gray stones forming the wall, the streets, and some of the houses. He pulled his jacket tighter, such a chill in the air.

"You haven't been here before?" Morgan seemed to sense the strangeness of the town as well.

"I don't know this place and I don't understand. I know where I'm going, Morgan." Night had yet to fall, and they passed several villagers going about their business. The gray theme of the town passed into their clothing. No color, everything was dull.

"They're sad." Morgan stepped closer. He wrapped an arm around her, drawing warmth from her even as the village tried to drag it from them.

"Where are the children?" He looked for them. There should be signs that they had been playing in the street. Their things should be scattered about as children did. No swings hung from trees in the yard. No toys rested against the front stoop. House after house, street after street, the light of childhood lacked. Tears burned in his chest, though he fought to keep them at bay.

"Look." Morgan pointed at the schoolhouse. Boards had been set across windows, barring the front door. White paint peeled from the wood siding.

"I cannot remain in this place. Is it any wonder my mind chooses to forget it?" Leave now. Urgency filled him.

"Dale, wait." Morgan pulled on his coat, but he jerked away, gathering the reins and lifting himself onto the horse.

"I cannot linger in this place, Morgan." No children. No music. No joy. How could any of them remain? Why did his stomach burn? He pressed the side of the horse with his heal. Morgan's voice whipped through the air streaming past, but he dared not turn back.

For it hadn't always been this way. He was almost certain. Memories that weren't really memories, they were more like ghosts of children playing ball in the street. A little girl chasing her brother as she squealed for her tortured doll. How could he have images in his brain of a place he'd never been? He kicked his horse into a gallop and prayed for relief.

~

Morgan watched him go. She could hear the

hooves of his horse picking up speed. The villagers mulling along the thoroughfare barely gave a glance in his direction. Barely glanced at her. She followed Dale at a sedate pace. How could the gray-clad villagers care so little about the world around them? The road turned uphill, leading away from the dour town into the woods. Gathering clouds deepened the shadows. She expected to see Dale around the corner, but there was no sign of him. Nor could she hear his horse. Morgan frowned, wrapped her cloak tighter against the drizzle starting to fall from the clouds, and plodded on.

Sometime later, she came upon him standing beside the path holding the leads.

He offered a sheepish grin. "I shouldn't have taken off like that."

She shrugged. "I don't think anyone noticed our coming or going."

"I found a shelter we can use. Rain is coming." A flash of lightning followed by thunder marked his words.

Morgan jumped from her mount and followed as the drizzle thickened to raindrops.

They sat beneath a lean-to with the horses lightly tethered to a branch.

"Where do we go from here?" Morgan asked as she stared into the driving rain. She could feel warmth emanating from Dale, but his quick abandon gave her pause. How well did she know him? Not at all. How far was she willing to trust him? She couldn't be certain.

"Across the river. The road leads through Chestershire, and then into the forest. Our home is there. My home."

"I don't recall it being so far."

He shrugged. "I cannot explain the memories. They are mixed up, like dreams in my head."

"We'll figure it out." Morgan placed her hand on his arm. She could feel tension harden his muscles. Could see his eyes darken.

The storm passed in the night and dawn greeted them with blue sky. The depression of the previous night seemed to have dissipated.

"What do we have for breakfast?" she asked.

Dale searched one of the bags and held up a loaf of bread. "I prefer to think it has raisins, and not something more unsavory."

"Too bad we've no cows around for milk." She sighed. "Is there anything other than water?"

"Apple cider." He tossed her a bag.

She tore off a piece of bread and tasted it. "Not a bad breakfast." She looked out from their shelter at the rain-washed path. "We did not get far yesterday. Will it be safe to travel this morning, or should we wait?"

"The trail leads on," he said as he shrugged. "Into the woods and to the foothills of the mountains. We are not likely to meet anyone."

Memory of the strange village from the previous day tightened her chest, but she wouldn't say anything about it. He'd probably already forgotten. "I'll need your help getting on the horse."

"I'm sure I can give you a hand." He grinned before finishing his bit of bread.

His good mood did not dissolve once they finished their meager breakfast and prepared to continue their journey. He bent, fingers entwined, to assist Morgan with her horse. Morgan lifted a leg, but then Dale straightened, and itched his head. She tilted her head.

He cleared his throat. "Sorry about that. Let's try it again."

She offered Dale an exasperating glance as he moved his hands once more, right when she was ready to step up.

He giggled. "It was an itch, couldn't be helped."

She wrinkled her nose. "Any more itches awaiting your attention?"

He wiggled as he pondered her words. "Nope. Feels like we are all good." Once more, he bent to provide her with the leverage she needed to mount her horse. And once more, his hands shifted out of the way. He laughed. "It is not I, but the world that moves beneath me." His blue eyes twinkled.

Morgan pressed her hands against her hips and tried to glare at him. "We will never reach our destination if the world continues to behave in such a way."

"I will not fail you this time, my lady." He offered a royal bow and set his hands to assist yet again. Morgan wrapped her hand around his collar. This time he allowed her foot to press against his linked hands and she lifted onto the horse.

He was soon mounted and ready to go. "Follow me."

She did, though her heart warred within her.

~

She wasn't too surprised when their path led them into another village. Dale at first paled, but then the sound of children playing brightened everything. They dismounted the horses to walk them through the gates. It was a small village with a winding road that followed the path of the river.

Dale pointed to where they could see the gate on the other side of town. "Straight through. We've no reason to linger here."

The children were curious about the pair of them and moved closer.

"This is life as it ought to be," Dale laughed as a gaggle of children ran around him and Morgan before chasing each other across the market. With a wide smile, he grabbed Morgan's hands and twirled her across the cobbled street. Morgan didn't notice her hood falling back, her attention held captive by Dale's bright eyes.

"Look at her hair!"

"She must be ancient."

"She doesn't look that old."

The murmurs of children playing in the streets cut through her pleasure. She slipped from Dale's arms and quickly lifted the cowl, covering her face with shadows.

"There is naught to fear." Dale drew her close although he spoke to the young ones.

"But where is her color?"

"Is she a witch?"

Dale's strong voice lifted with the sound of laughter. "She is a child of God, as we all are. There is no evil in her."

Morgan felt the warmth of his hand against her cheek. She looked at him, unable to hide the tears in her eyes.

"Why do you hide from them? You are beautiful."

"I am colorless."

"Does the moon lack color? Is there shame in the silvery light that brightens the darkness? The witch may have taken something from you, Morgan. But she did not take you."

His hand moved to her cloak. She stood with him in the middle of the street, in his arms, as he pulled the cover away from her. Her face heated, but it was the intense gleam of his eyes rather than embarrassment. His attention, in that moment, focused entirely on her, and Morgan knew she would offer her life to save his.

The sounds of the market drew them apart, although Dale kept hold of her hand. Morgan offered a sweet smile as she swung his arm back and forth.

"Ah, I smell roast mutton. Shall we stop for lunch?" Dale drew her to an inn across from the market. They joined a table with a farmer and his wife.

~

The smell of steak and mushroom pie lingered in the air. Morgan thought Dale would attack it with gusto, but he seemed more pensive, though an odd light burned in his eyes as he watched the children. The farmer tried to get him to talk, but he would not be distracted.

Morgan pressed her hand against his. "Eat. We need strength for the day. This is much better than the bread you still have in your bags."

Her touch drew his attention. He shook himself and bit into the pie. Moments later, he'd slipped back into watching, his foot tapping to some unseen music. With a sigh, Morgan finished her meal and stood. She thanked the farmer and his wife for sharing space with them, and then she glanced at Dale. "We should leave. You do not know if we will be able to reach your home before nightfall."

He pushed away from the table, eager to move.

They hadn't gone far when he pulled her into an alley. "Something is happening." He held his hands toward her. She laid her small ones on top of his and he wrapped his hands around them.

She shivered. There was no warmth in his fingers. "What is wrong?"

"Something is happening to me. I want to play my flute." He moved his fingers as though he were already creating a melody. "Follow me, Morgan. Stay with me. Even if I don't want you to."

Morgan drew her hands from his and placed them on his cheeks. "I won't leave you." Her promise came with a kiss. The warmth of his breath, and then her lips against his, drove the cold from him for a moment. He pulled her closer, deepening the kiss. Love for Dale burgeoned through the confusing memories and feelings that warred within her. Breathless, they parted. He rested his forehead against hers.

Morgan felt her chest tighten. "I won't ever leave you again."

"I must go." Dale spoke, his eyes swirling with an eerie light, and then he pushed her away and ran from the alley.

Though his abrupt departure startled her, Morgan spun around and followed. Doubts that had consumed her as they waited out the storm no longer mattered. Her heart chose to trust him. She went to follow him into the tavern, but he burst through the doors. He had removed his jacket. His white shirt open at the neck revealed a patch of dark hair upon his chest. He paid her no heed, though he sprinted past with his camel breaches tucked into his boots. He lifted his flute to his mouth and began to play.

Instantly, the street transformed. Children ran to join him, transfixed by the elegant notes weaving through the cool air. He played for them. Bowing to reveal his fingers dancing across the holes drilled through the wood. Chasing them. Running from them. He fell to the ground, and they piled upon him. His laughter filled the space between notes.

Morgan couldn't fathom what had come over him. He frolicked like a child, charming them and drawing them to him. She drove through the mass of bodies to help him rise, but his eyes showed no recognition. He ignored her hand, bouncing to his feet on his own. He continued to play. Children of all ages followed as he skipped along the main street. They passed the houses that opened to the fields and farms. Voices filled the air, jubilant in their sounds. Two small hands tugged her forward, bade her to join them.

Dale played through the streets, turning into a field, and leading them away. Is this what had happened in Wyrwhith? At least two dozen children followed the sound of the flute. She turned back, but the village was no longer in view. The children tugged against her hands. Two faces, one a boy of about six and the other a girl slightly younger, looked up at her as they pulled to get away. Mist chilled her feet, rising to engulf them. More and more children appeared in the mist. They milled aimlessly, staring at Dale. She could still hear the flute trilling through the fog. The little ones slipped from her hands. A young girl stood a few feet away. She looked at Dale, but she also glanced at her. Morgan's breath caught in her throat. Red hair like her own. The apron that had once been hers. No, it couldn't be…

"Angel?" Morgan fell to her knees beside the child. Freckles across her nose. Butterfly birthmark by her right ear. She grabbed Angel by the waist. The child's attention remained with Dale, her feet bouncing to the music. Others danced and ran around him. What had he done? What had he become? Morgan sobbed as her heart chilled. She turned back to Angel. How could she have forgotten? Lived so long without remembering her sister?

"Angel, look at me!" Her hands gripped the coarse fabric of Angel's dress. She shook her. "Wake up," her voice choked. "Father and Mother need you to come home. I need you. Angel, how could I have forgotten?'"

The body beneath her hands strained, struggled to get away from her. Angel stared at Dale.

"No, Angel. You don't have to go. Be free of him. Come home with me. Angel, please. Wake up."

Angel blinked as she turned her face to Morgan. Her brows drew close. "Don't cry, Sissie."

Morgan couldn't stop the tears. "Angel."

"I have to go," she tried once more to pull away.

"You mustn't. Come home with me. To your family. We need you."

Her eyes looked sad. "This is where I belong."

"How can I save you?"

"You cannot. She is too powerful."

"The witch? There has to be a way to stop her."

"There's an old man on the river. He knows something." Angel began to cry. "At least I think... he's seen us."

Morgan wanted to pull her close, but Angel slipped away. The music stilled. Children stopped, grew silent. The fog lifted as an eerie quiet settled across the hill. When the mist had cleared, only two of them remained. Herself, and Dale.

"What have you done?" Morgan ran at him, fists flying against his chest. "You stole them. You stole all of them." She knocked the flute from his hand. He pushed her away to retrieve the instrument.

"What are you talking about?"

"The children were here. You led them here with your music. But there were others as well. My sister." She hit him again. He grabbed her hands.

"I don't know…"

"You." How could her body betray her? To want the feel of his hands on her? "Angel disappeared." She closed her eyes against the onslaught of memories. "They sent me to my grandparents, but many of the children in the village disappeared. How could I have forgotten for so long?"

"It wasn't me," Dale shook his head.

She twisted in his arms. "I saw you. I witnessed it myself. You can't say it wasn't you. Where are they? Where are the children? Where is Angel?"

"I don't know. The last thing I remember is being in the village." He looked around them at the hills dotted with large oak trees whose long branches swayed towards the ground. "Why are we here? This isn't the right path to home." He rubbed his head.

Morgan pushed against his chest. "No, you led them here to take them. Is that why you led me to the witch? To be rid of me?"

He rubbed his head. "I would never harm anyone. Not you, and certainly not children. I wouldn't. Couldn't."

"You did." Tears pained her throat and her hits against his chest weakened. "Where are they? They were here and now they are gone. The villagers will come for you. They will kill you."

"Then the children will be lost forever."

She jerked out of his arms. "Angel spoke of an old man by the river. We visit him first."

Dale didn't argue.

Morgan moved from him. "I will get the horses. You wait by the road." Would he be there, or would he run, the coward?

~

Dale paced at the side of the road. They had gone into the town. Had tavern food, though he didn't recall eating much. Children were playing in the alley. But what happened after? Why was Morgan furious with him? And Angel, her sister? He fought to remember. She'd been much younger. He remembered a toddler stumbling through the house. What had happened to her?

The sound of horses drew his attention. Morgan sat, back straight, face firm. Gone was the affection, the comradery. Here was a woman who had learnt pain. He mounted the horse without a word.

"We go to the river. The stable master had a vague notion of an old man who lives near the water." Morgan took the lead.

Dale followed, watching her. Tendrils of white waved through the air. She turned, and soon they were encompassed by trees. Eventually they came to a little hut a few yards from the flowing waters of a river.

Shack was a kind description of the old fisherman's house. Boards dried, beaten, and warped by weather and age formed the mishmash of walls that kept it from falling over. Barely. The old man rose from his rocker as he spied their arrival. He held a rod in his hand and looked as though he was about to take the boat onto the river.

He nodded and listened as Morgan explained their quest. "A witch, you say?"

Morgan nodded as she gripped the rein of the horse in her hand. "My sister said you could help us be rid of her. You've seen them. You can help us save the children."

He frowned, glancing past them into the woods that surrounded his home. "Are there children who need saving?"

"She stole them. We have been in three villages we know of. There are likely others."

The old man shook his head. "You will need to ask her the purpose for the children. That is a question I cannot answer."

"How do we free them from her power?" She watched as he moved closer to the edge of the river.

"Destroy the witch, of course." He leaned his rod against a tree and hooked a worm. "There is little else you can do."

"What of Dale?" She glanced at the silent man sitting on his horse beside her. "With the part he has played in this, will he be saved as well?"

The old man stared at her. His eyes were the color of pine needles. "Will you? Is there a way to regain what has been lost? You must wait and see."

"You waste time." Morgan snapped, and then covered her eyes. "I apologize. I did not mean to be rude. I weary of this journey."

"Three things you must look for. Three. One of them may be the means of destroying her. First, there is something precious to her that will need to be broken. Second, put her house to fire. But be warned, you will never regain what has been lost if you destroy it. Third, there is starlight glass. One who has been in the power of the witch must open it."

"What happens when we do?"

He shrugged. "Whatever must be done. That is the way of it."

The old man dropped his fishing gear into the boat and pushed the bow from the river's edge. He jumped in and went away.

Dale moved off his horse and stood beside her. "What's happened? Where is he going?"

Morgan stared at the disappearing boat. Had he been helpful? Three things that might work. She closed her eyes, putting the three items to memory.

"Morgan?"

She turned from him with a glare. "We waste time. Lead me to the witch's lair."

"Is there naught we can do?"

Morgan didn't bother with an answer. She raised

her brows and waited for him to do what she had said. He was both man and boy and she could both love and hate him.

~

It took another day for them to find the witch's house. The woods turned cold. The chatter of birds silenced. The path narrowed with little chance to go any other way. When they crossed into the clearing, Morgan swallowed the lump in her throat. Much remained the same, except more parts of the house were now vibrant colors. She pushed her hands into her pockets to keep from touching her hair when she saw the red door.

"Do you remember when we came upon it the first time?" Morgan stepped closer to Dale.

He nodded. His face was tight with pain. "But I also remember playing in the garden as a boy."

"She planted those memories to make you stay. To do her bidding."

"Then it is time to be rid of them." He walked closer.

"You have returned, my son." An older woman moved across the porch.

Morgan shook. She remembered the feel of those hands. Her cold eyes. Morgan grabbed Dale's hand. His warmth chased away the chill of fear.

"Who have you brought home with you? Have you found yourself a young woman?"

"She is an old friend."

The witch came down the stairs.

"Old friend? I do not remember such a one as this."

Morgan pulled her hood down. "Mayhap you

will now."

Dale squeezed her hand.

The witch gasped. "My goodness, I do remember you."

Morgan straightened. "We have come to stop you. To save the children."

"Are children in trouble?" The witch searched around the clearing and the side of the house that was in view. "Why do you come here?"

"You are the one who has them. You've used Dale to draw them from their homes."

"There are no children here, foolish girl." She lifted her hands. "My son is grown, as you can see."

Dale tugged Morgan's hand. "Why don't we go inside? Have tea and make some sense of things."

"Yes, do come in." The witch beckoned to them. "I have a fresh fruitcake cooling on the counter."

Morgan did not want to enter the house. But the old man's words compelled her. She would not find something precious to the witch outside. She allowed Dale to lead her up the steps, across the porch, and through the open door.

The house was bright and well-tended. She could smell the mixture of cinnamon and oranges in the air. There were a few knickknacks lying about, cases of books, fresh flowers and dry sprigs.

"Have you no compliment for me, my dear?" The witch stood in the kitchen smiling at her.

Morgan swallowed. "Um, it is a lovely house." For all its cute comfort, the house crawled with unseen menace. Morgan felt it like tiny spiders crawling across her skin.

The witch puzzled. "You did not expect my

house to be pleasant?"

"No, ma'am, I did not."

"Things are not always as they seem." She pulled cups and saucers from a cupboard and placed them on a tray. "You think you know my son, and yet, how is that possible?"

Morgan's mind whirled. Something unseen worked within the walls of the house, trying to make her forget. She closed her eyes. The image of Angel strengthened her resolve. That memory remained strong, of holding her sister and then having her ripped from her arms. Pain and sadness were real. She opened her eyes.

"Tea?" The witch held a tea pot above a cup, poised to pour. It was a green tea pot that made Morgan feel ill to look upon.

Dale still held her hand. He tugged her toward the table. She pulled back, unbalancing him. He knocked into the witch, causing her to drop the pot. The sound of shattering pottery crashed through the room.

"What have you done?" the witch hissed.

"I am sorry," he said as he danced away from the spilled tea spreading across the tile floor. "I will clean it up."

"No. Leave it be." The witch's voice hardened. "Take your guest outside."

Had that been precious to her? Morgan wondered, but nothing seemed different. Dale tugged her toward the front door.

Morgan paused, glancing around. "Does your mother," calling her that left a bitter taste in her mouth. "Does she have a starlight glass?"

"Starlight?" Dale seemed confused for a moment, but then his face brightened. "Do you mean the lantern that can be used at night?"

"It could be." Morgan shrugged. "Where does she keep it?"

He looked at the stairs to the loft.

Morgan placed her hand on his arm. "Please, Dale. We need it."

It took little time for him to retrieve. The object looked like a spherical ball of glass held in a net.

"What are you doing?"

Dale started at the witch's tone. He flushed and swung around. Morgan tried to stop him, but his elbow struck a candle. Instead of snuffing out when it hit the floor, the flame lit the curtain and fire blazed to life.

"Not the house," Morgan rushed forward to pull the drapes from the window. She fell into the witch who had moved as well.

The house caught fire, as did the witch. Her morning gown burst into flame. Dale grabbed Morgan, lifting her off her feet. She buried her head in his shoulder as the cries of the old woman mingled with the roar of the fire. She felt a breath of air as they exited. Across the garden, he dropped to his knees. Morgan turned to look. The house was engulfed. How could it have spread so quickly? Dale groaned beside her. His hands covered his face as he bent forward. She placed a hand on his back. If the spell were broken, he would not grieve the woman he thought to be his mother. But his body shook, and he fell against her. She wrapped her arms around him. Was the witch not dead? They could no longer hear her cries. What about the children? Tears poured down her face. The colors of the house burned up with the flames and smoke. There would be no recovering that part of herself.

She leaned her head against his. "Where is the starlight glass?"

"What good is it to us?" His voice sounded husky.

"The old man at the river said three things could break the spell. Breaking something of hers. Burning the house. Or using the starlight glass."

"You told me nothing of this."

"I could not. You did not wish to see the children restored. Or the witch destroyed."

"You don't understand what I suffer." He dropped his head into his hands. "Knowing some things in my mind are real. Other thoughts are false. You have taken so much. How do I know you are not false as well?"

Morgan shook him. "Burning the house took from me any chance of restoring what the witch stole."

"What will the starlight do?"

"I don't know. Someone who has been in the witch's power must open it."

He offered her the sphere, but she shook her head. "You had more time within her power. You open it."

He removed the sphere from the net, holding it in his hand. Sparkles of sunlight danced on the ground beside them. Morgan wanted to touch it, and yet she sensed she should not.

"What do I with it?" Dale asked.

"Break it?"

He moved to the stone fence that closed in the garden. Morgan remained kneeling on the ground, watching. He raised his arm, looked at the smoldering remains of the house, and threw the starlight glass at the rock. Shattering glass pulsed through the garden. He remained transfixed. For a moment, nothing happened, then light arched out from the rocks followed by a thick mist. Dale fell.

"Dale," Morgan cried as she jumped to her feet and ran to his side. "Dale," she whispered his name, grabbing his hand as his body convulsed. His hand crushed hers, but she did not try to release him. She pressed her other hand against his forehead, brushing through his hair. She felt shadows brushing against her in the mist. His body relaxed, but he did not open his eyes. The fog around them began to swirl. She moved her hands to his chest, shaking him. "Dale." He did not respond. She leaned over him, holding him as the wind blew against her. Something slammed against her, and she knew no more.

~

"The boat, Morgan. The boat." Dale urgently cried.

Morgan shook herself. Something had just happened. Something important. The boat she had built with Dale bobbed on the water, further and further from shore. That didn't matter. She looked at her hands. Looked at Dale.

Dale watched her. "What is it?"

For a moment, the image of a man imposed itself over her childhood friend. Then a bird squawked. A strange bird with a beautiful blue tail.

"Have you seen the like?" Dale asked, but she placed her hand on his arm to prevent him from stepping closer to it. He turned to her.

Morgan felt cold slither against her skin as she peered at the bird. Bad things would happen if they followed it. She didn't know how she knew, but she felt certain of the truth. She turned her back on it. "Let us stay with the boat. I do not wish our labor to be in vain."

He grinned, a boyish charming grin. "As if anything with you would be labor. Come, the boat will put to shore somewhere. We follow the river."

This is what she wanted. Her heart lightened, as though a mysterious burden dissipated. Dale noticed something. He curled one of her red locks around his finger. Kissed her cheek somewhere near her mouth. They moved forward. Someday he wouldn't miss. She was certain of it.

Beast

(Based on the fairytale Beauty and the Beast)

Tales of a young woman marrying an animal groom that transforms into a handsome man have been around for centuries. A French collection of tales, called The Young American and tales of the Sea, is the first written account of *Beauty and the Beast*. Since that time, the story of the enchanted prince and the beguiled heroine has been taken onto the stage and movie screens (thanks to Disney). I've grown up hearing the story multiple times, which is probably where the retelling of such a tale comes from. Please, enjoy.

LAURIE LEE

ONE

O nce upon a time in a country much like England before machines ran on their own and smog poisoned the air, was the realm of Hwelsham. Birds flying over the land could see the curling river and the road that followed it, the forest that covered the hills, and the valleys between with small villages. Beyond the hills came flatlands, perfect for farming when the high sun cast off winter's cloak. Great manors controlled the farming lands, and the small villages that grew nearby provided workers.

Nimglen was such a manor. Thick stones piled on one another formed the main house which could easily sleep a party of four and twenty in their own rooms. Green moss and lichens grew along the mortar, giving it an abandoned air; and yet, the curtains moved, candlelight flickered from upper windows, and on a cold evening, wisps of gray smoke floated into the night sky, filling the nearby fields with the scent of applewood and old tobacco. Farmers worked the fields of Nimglen with pay regularly offered to them. Yet the master of the manor hadn't been seen in years. Perhaps, that is how the stories grew.

Just outside the region of Nimglen, too close to the woods to be good for farming, lay the village of Bakersfield. Rather than farming, a good portion of its welfare came from the bakers. As one would visit Smithville for ironworkers, and Seamsville for the finest in clothing, Bakersfield housed the best bakers of Hwelsham. On Fridays before market, the air shimmered with sweetbreads and pies baking in the ovens. Birds would laze in the trees, drunk on the scent of apples and spice.

In the village of Bakersfield, lived a father with three daughters. He was a good sort of man, neither rich nor poor, neither powerful nor slave to any other. Selwyn Orcroft wasn't a baker. He took the goods produced in the village and distributed them across Hwelsham depending on where requests were made. His daughters, being of an age to take care of themselves, sometimes made requests of him—to find on his travels such things as fabrics, tools, plants, and the like.

TWO

Gladra, the eldest of the three daughters, leaned against the kitchen doorway. "Looks like fine weather for the next week."

"Have you turned your interests to the skies?" Selwyn teased.

"I have many interests, no thanks to your influence." Gladra grinned, and then noticed Torsa, a few years younger than herself, reclining on a simple lounge near the window. Gladra recognized the gleam in her sister's eye. Torsa was up to something, usually trouble. She glanced back at Selwyn, reposing against the mantle as he smoked his pipe. The sweet tinge of Cavendish added to the comfortable room with its cheery yellow walls. Selwyn's wavy light brown hair needed a trim, but the late spring season kept him busy. "Will you be gone long?"

"Not more than usual."

Torsa perked up. "If you arrive in Wellsford by Saturday morn, you can shop the market."

He laughed. "Is it to be one of those journeys? I've goods to deliver across the valley."

"Would you father?" Ora, the youngest of them

at thirteen, straightened from her place at the small table beside the window. With hair the same color as Selwyn but curlier, large blue eyes, and an easy smile, Ora would be the beauty of the three sisters. Torsa had a similar look to Ora, but Torsa cared more for books and learning, not taking the time to fix her hair or arrange her outfits to best suit the slender Orcroft visage. Gladra looked on her sisters with affection.

Selwyn nodded at Ora's question, and her cry of delight was sufficient for them all. He laughed. "What would you have?"

Ora dropped the needle she'd been holding above a crocheting pattern of an owl in a blue tree. "Do you think they would have a jeweler?"

Selwyn grinned. "Would you desire a diamond or a ruby?"

Ora blushed. "Nothing so grand. A gold pendant with a pretty chain, perhaps?"

He nodded, then used the end of his pipe to point at Gladra. "What for you, eldest?"

Pretty jewels had little use for her. With her father's strong facial features more so than her mother's, one would be hard-pressed to call Gladra pretty. Adornments wouldn't change anything. But there was something she desired. "If you are sure, a group of Elves forge in the lower hills. I hear they sell their wares at Wellsford. I long for a blade, a light silver blade. If you could."

"An Elven blade for my silver-haired elf?"

She nodded, not minding the reference to her silvery blond hair. Mother's hair had been like hers as well, if she remembered correctly.

Selwyn looked at Torsa. "This is your idea. What would you have?"

Torsa twirled a lock of her blond hair around her finger. "Now that I've thought about it, Father, I desire something altogether different. A rose, a beautifully blooming rose."

"From a flower vendor?"

She crinkled her nose. "Not from a vendor. Those roses would be cut and starting to wilt. No. It must be a fresh rose in perfect bloom."

Gladra gave her sister a puzzled look. Did she mean to plant the rose in their garden? Why did something strange seem to be at work with her request?

"A blossom for my bookworm?" Selwyn didn't seem bothered at all. He grinned, returning to smoking his pipe. He would try to find her the perfect rose.

Gladra looked at Torsa. The girl positively beamed with contentment. Odd.

THREE

Selwyn intended to return by the sixth day. On the seventh day, Gladra paced the halls of their modest house. The rose carpet that lined the hallway was already worn thin. The back kitchen had been cleaned. She'd tried to get Torsa and Ora to straighten their bedrooms on the second floor, but the chore wasn't likely to be accomplished anytime soon. When night settled without news, she reassured her sisters. Selwyn applied himself to obtaining their gifts. He'd be home or a note sent round by the following morning.

A note arrived just a few hours after the sun had risen from its slumber, but Gladra hadn't slipped into sleep until the wee hours of the night and so tripped getting out of bed at the sound of the bell. She heard Torsa and saw her holding the note with a gleeful look on her face. Gladra waited impatiently with her heart in her throat, longing to tear the note from her sister's hands. "What does it say?"

"Father asks me to join him."

Gladra frowned. "You? Where?

"Not that far." Torsa gave Gladra a look. "He stays at Nimglen."

"Nimglen?" Gladra wrapped her arms around herself. Why did even saying the name of the manor make her want to shake?

Torsa bounced on the balls of her feet. "I can go on my own and take the carriage. Perhaps Father has an injury."

Gladra hated herself for considering it. "It is too dangerous on your own. Why would he call for only you?" Gladra reached for the note.

Torsa crumpled it in her hand. "Nonsense. I've travelled beyond town on my own before. If I leave now, we'll be back before the sun begins to set."

"Bessie couldn't handle more than two of you in the carriage." Gladra didn't really want to travel. Considering the horse was a kind thought, wasn't it?

Torsa offered a comforting hug. "I'll go and bring Father back. It will be fine, you'll see."

FOUR

Except it wasn't. Selwyn returned, as promised, in the carriage late that afternoon. Gladra ran to help him, taking a rose he held out to her. He didn't say a word as he pulled himself down the two steps to the ground and shuffled to the house.

Poor Selwyn. His skin had turned ashen; his eyes swam with weariness and pain. His shoulders drooped with weight though he let his bag hit the floor beside the front doorway. The sword she requested lay within the bag. The end of the chain for Ora dangled from it. In Gladra's hand lay Torsa's blood red rose, still fresh and vibrant as the day it had been cut. He took it back from her, laid it upon a silver platter on the buffet in the dining room, and placed a glass over it. Gladra blinked, then faced outside the front door once more. The carriage was empty. How could that be? Where was Torsa?

He rubbed his eyes. "She is safe. Visiting for a while."

"Visiting who?" Gladra's throat hurt, and the question came out more like a squeak.

But Selwyn shook his head. "She is safe," he

repeated, and refused to say more.

The house felt wrong. Dinner was upon the table, but none could eat. Selwyn did not speak, and Ora became weepy without knowing why. The rosemary potatoes were hard, and the lump of meat resembled something best left in the field. How was Gladra supposed to focus on cooking when her heart was so burdened? She battled sore thoughts as the evening progressed slowly. What if the three of them had joined Selwyn, instead of Torsa going alone? What then?

Earlier than necessary, she retired to her bedroom. From her bed, she watched a quarter moon hang outside the window facing toward the west. Facing toward Nimglen. Something tugged her in that direction. It had to be Torsa. Why else would she be drawn to a place she'd never seen? She closed her eyes and fell into an uneasy sleep riddled with shadows.

Why indeed. For what Gladra didn't know and couldn't imagine was that a curse lay upon Nimglen, and here finally was one who could break it. Not the girl who had come to stay at Nimglen, but a close relative. The curse reached for the close relative even as it reached for the one who had created the curse in the first place. One would destroy the other, it was just a matter of who.

FIVE

C old stone beneath Gladra's bare feet startled her. She stood just inside a stone fence watching her father struggle to crawl over it. Over it? Why would he sneak into such a place? She looked around. The garden was not well-tended. Bushes closest to the massive manor were dead. Only those nearest the fence beckoned with blooms larger than her hands in colors like burgundy, crimson, and yellow. Selwyn gave a nervous glance at the house but walked the path around the roses until he stopped to make his choice.

Gladra saw movement from within the house. Though she cried out, the sound of her voice gave no pause to her father's actions. Nor did it cause the creature striding through the wasted, untended spoils of a dead garden to pause. He was a man bound up within a monster. Looking at them both made her dizzy, but that didn't explain how her heart lurched within her chest. The beast-man paused, its nostrils flaring as though searching for the scent of something it could not see, before continuing to move toward Selwyn.

Gladra found herself within the house. Selwyn

sat on a chair, a glass of brandy in his shaking hand. The beast paced the marble floors, growling about something she couldn't quite grasp. Then Selwyn was leaning over the table, scrawling his note.

Time passed swiftly, the sun set and rose as Gladra stood for what only seemed like minutes. Suddenly, Torsa stood beside Selwyn. "Let me stay. It is my mess." Her younger sister's voice wobbled.

Gladra gave herself a shake. *What had happened? Was happening?* She looked at the beast man. He watched Torsa with hungry eyes. Not an evil look, but needy. Torsa snuck a few glances, but her attention focused on other things in the room. Gladra frowned. Why didn't Torsa seem surprised to be there?

"You tried, Father." Torsa murmured as she held his arm.

Gladra saw him tremble. His lower chin quivered. Then Torsa faced the beast.

"I will remain with you, but you must allow our father to return home. The children cannot survive without him. We have no mother."

Children? What children? Ora was thirteen already and Gladra almost twenty.

Spittle soaked the deep ridges that bordered its mouth, and its beady eyes traveled from Torsa to her father and back. His jaw lowered and a panting growl emanated from its mouth. Gladra felt her stomach quiver. The beast walked on two legs and dressed as a man. The white long sleeve shirt hung open to its chest revealing thick muscles covered with dark coarse hair. Its legs were draped in loose fitting trousers, but the bare feet were wolfish with long claws. The gentleman-like manner of the beast whispered where its wild nature roared.

Torsa paled but faced the beast. "I'll stay," she repeated, though no smile tempered her face this time.

Selwyn shook his head. "No. You return to the others. I can provide…"

"She stays." The beast spoke deep from his chest. Gladra wondered if she hadn't been in a dream could she have felt the sound of his voice moving through the floor.

Torsa crossed her arms. "Unharmed and unhindered. Promise my father that."

He looked at them both and nodded. "I promise. Unharmed and unhindered. She stays."

"For how long?" Selwyn whispered, the edge of fear evident in his voice.

"Until it is done," it grunted. "Take the rose. Its price is paid."

"Go Father, while light remains." She placed her hands on his arm.

"Torsa." He drew her close for a moment. His tears dampened her cheek, and he stepped away. His feet moved him across the marble squares, through the arched doorway, and then he disappeared. Gladra wanted to scream at him to turn back. He couldn't mean to leave Torsa with it. She looked at the beast, but it watched Torsa walk away. The beast man stood in the middle of the room, and Gladra snuffed away compassion for it. What right did it have to demand Torsa remain at Nimglen? Finally, it growled and sauntered in the opposite direction.

The vision faded and Gladra woke shaking.

Tears dripped down her cheek. She was the eldest child. When Mother died, most of the responsibility for her two younger sisters fell to her shoulders. Anger stirred among the other emotions, ruining her sleep.

Making a decision spurred her to action. She dressed swiftly. A few minutes later, Gladra pressed the final button through the last hole of her leather vest that wrapped around her beige chemise. She pulled at the waist, adjusting the fit. The split skirt in green was full but allowed her to move more easily. Selwyn had taught her to fence, and she'd demonstrated a talent for it. A talent the beast would soon feel. She strapped the slim scabbard with her new elven blade to her side. The unusual weight at her hip unbalanced her walk. She tested drawing the sword and brandished it easily. Orange hues lit bits of clouds close to the eastern horizon as she walked from the house. Mist clung like ghosts to the edges of the village. Gladra swallowed fear as she saddled Bessie and took to the road.

Another saw her coming as a vision of doom. The witch, too far and weakened by the woman whose presence already snapped at the delicate weavings of the spell, sought a means to bring the interlude to an end. A permanent end.

SIX

T he ride to Nimglen was slow in the fog. Gladra rubbed Bessie's side as she encouraged her to keep to the road. Even as daylight brightened, the fog remained their companion. Several hours passed before she made the turn toward the manor. Though she'd never seen the actual building, she knew where Nimglen was. There was the stone wall with roses peaking over the top. That must have been what drew Selwyn for Torsa's strange request.

Gladra moved Bessie close to the wall. "Stay still," she muttered to her horse and then lifted herself high enough to grasp the top of the wall. She wobbled and hugged the wall. Determined not to give way to fear, she pulled herself to where she could go over the top. Her sword jangled as she landed in a soft patch beside a tree.

Silence, like an expectant hush, surrounded her. The sky overhead was hazy. Gladra brushed dirt from her vest. Her skin tingled. Where was Torsa? Would she be alright? She stepped out from beneath the tree. The manor loomed to her left. It was so big. What of the beast that lived in it?

She did not have to wonder for long. Gladra felt her heart move in her chest once more as she glimpsed it. He lurched from a doorway at the side of the house. Fear shook her hands, and she gripped the handle of the sword. His eyes looked at her hand, and it snarled. Gladra barely had time to pull the sword from its holder. The beast had its own weapon. She stumbled through the first moves but managed to stay out of its way.

He growled at her. "This is not your place. Why have you trespassed?"

How dare he speak of trespass when her sister was held against her will? Blind fury gripped her, and she swung wildly with the blade.

He parried her attack, his blade ringing against hers. With height greater than her own he blocked her attempt to retreat. Chest heaving, Gladra held her sword toward him and kept the stone wall at her back.

"The time has come to kill the beast?" He snarled, swinging his thicker blade in an arc.

"I would free my sister."

"Free?" He lowered the sword with another snarl. "She came of her own volition and stays of her own free will. Torsa is no prisoner."

"Is she not?" Gladra raised her chin. "Then bring her to me, allow me to return with her to my father's house."

"She stays," the beast screamed.

Gladra refused to back away though her fingers shook, and the muscles of her arms ached with the effort it took to keep a grasp on the weapon. "That is what you call free?" Something other than fear stirred her. Though anger gave a red glow to his features, the eyes of the beast were not those of an animal. They were human.

He lowered his arm. "This fight is not yours."

"Not mine?" She actually took a step closer to him. "She is family, of my own flesh and blood. I will not leave her here to rot."

"Your sister chose, what right is it of yours to question that?" It spat.

Gladra moved closer still as fury burned within her. "The choice being our father or herself to remain as captive? What else could she do?"

Its eyes flared, and then of a sudden, the rage faded. "I weary of your meddling. Find you sister and speak with her yourself. But she remains until I release her." With a grunt, he spun on his heel and walked across the garden.

Gladra wasn't ready for him to walk away. She followed, her small footsteps prancing to keep up. She could almost touch the white shirt covering his back when he swerved around to face her once more. Gladra gasped as pain seared her side. Somehow, she'd been impaled on his sword. Horror darkened his features, but his eyes captured her attention as darkness swirled around her. "Your eyes," she gasped and then lost consciousness.

No one was around to hear the howl of the witch as she faced her failure in the crystal ball. The girl should have died, not release him even further from the curse. The sight of roses across the garden bursting into bloom hurt her eyes. She must hurry.

SEVEN

Gladra stretched an arm above her head, wondering as she sank into a soft mattress. She savored the unusual comfort, but then something within jarred her. They had no mattresses—she moved, and pain ripped through her side. She gasped. A sob sounded from the shadows. Someone pressed against the bed, grabbing hold of Gladra's hand. She turned her head and frowned at Torsa. "What are you doing here?"

"What were you thinking?" Torsa sobbed as she knelt beside Gladra.

Gladra offered a weak smile. "What happened?"

"You don't remember? It hurt you, tried to kill you. And then fever has raged for days. What would I have done if you…"

Gladra patted Torsa's hand, silencing her. "Not your fault. Not its fault either. His, I mean." She tried to take a breath and pain seared her side. She used shallower breaths.

Torsa brushed hair from Gladra's face. "How can you say that? The leather from your vest saved your life. It would have taken it."

"Where is he?"

"I haven't seen him." Torsa scowled. "Not for days. He brought something to break the fever. I waited to use it. I don't think it can be trusted. "

Gladra closed her eyes and breathed. "The medicine worked?"

"Or I waited long enough for the worst to pass, and it couldn't harm you."

Sleep pulled at her, but Gladra didn't mind. She dreamt of eyes, surprisingly human for a beast.

The last tendrils of the spell clung to Nimglen, feeding the black fever that kept the girl from connecting with the man. The witch was ever so close, another day or two and she could finish the matter. She touched the crystal ball and wove the black fever into the beast as well, even as she sickened the roses that had dared bloom. "You think you know despair?" She touched the figure that looked more man than beast. "Wait for me."

EIGHT

T he following day, Gladra felt well enough to get up from the bed. She stretched to the left. The wound hurt, but not so much as to keep her down. She washed in cold water and dressed for the day.

Torsa grabbed her in the hallway. "Something is wrong." She kept hold of Gladra's hand and pulled her through the hallway to a room on the end. Heavy curtains had been pulled back, allowing light into the room. A man lay on the floor.

Gladra ran to his side, ignoring the pain in her side as she dropped to her knees. "What has happened to him?"

"I don't know." Torsa knelt beside Gladra.

Gladra pulled him gently over. It was him, but no longer a beastly form. He was deathly pale. She opened his shirt and laid her ear against his chest. She could discern a slight beat. "He lives." She looked at her sister with delight. "We must move him to a bed."

He was heavy. Much heavier than either of them could carry. They pulled him closer to the bed but were unable to lift him off the floor. "Hand me a pillow." Gladra raised his head, then set it upon the cushion.

Torsa moved to stand at the window. "The garden is dead."

"What?" Gladra ran to her side. They both looked at the man on the floor.

"This is my fault," Torsa blinked tears from her eyes. "I thought…"

Gladra placed her hand on Torsa's arm, encouraging her to continue, but her younger sister flushed and stared at the ground. "What did you do?" Unease caused her stomach to turn as Gladra waited for her sister to respond.

"I read about him in old tales." Her voice scratched with sobs. "He was ugly and mean and he'd been hiding here forever. I knew if Father crossed the garden he would be made to stay, if the beast still lived. I could switch places." She buried her face in her arms.

Gladra moved to the man. Her side ached, but the wound had been an accident. She touched his cold skin, smooth without the beastly mange. What had happened to change him back? And why was he dying? "Why did you want to come here?"

"I'm sorry. It's my fault, isn't it?" Torsa whispered. She sat at the edge of the bed, by his feet. She wiped her nose with her sleeve. "His feet are dirty."

Muddy, as though he'd walked in the garden. Gladra wondered, and then she lifted one of his hands. "Dirt, and thorn pricks." She met her sister's glance. "He was searching for something."

"In the dead garden? But what?"

"A rose." She swept his long, obsidian hair from

his face. "You needed a rose, but they were dead." His eyes didn't open, but breath moved through him still.

"Why is he not dead yet?"

Gladra looked up at her sister. "Because a rose survives."

"The one father brought home for me." Excitement stirred the air. Torsa jumped to her feet. "I will ride for it and bring it back."

Gladra shook her head. "I will go."

Torsa disagreed. "I am faster on a horse. Remain with him. He changed when he met you. I will return with the flower, and you can save him."

She ran from the room before Gladra could argue further. With a grunt of irritation, she pulled a cushion close to the makeshift bed on the floor. She wrapped her hands around his, praying warmth from her body would sustain him. "She will return, I promise." She chafed his hand, and held it close to her body. "Whatever ill plan she started with, she is sorry. Don't die. Wait for us. Don't die."

Afternoon light began to fade from the room. Gladra roused herself long enough to find candles and matches and pull together a platter of cold food and water for her supper. She dribbled water into his mouth and felt her heart leap with joy when he swallowed. But he did not wake. She tucked a blanket around his body, slumped across a chaise nearby, and continued to wait.

A rattle of breath and choking roused her in early morning. She ran to his side, turning him slightly and pounding on his back. "No, you don't." His coughing subsided and she lay him flat once more. She wrestled another pillow to elevate his head. "For being on death's door, you're not all light and feathery." She gasped as she released him. She kissed his forehead. "Do not die on me now, beastly man. Help will arrive soon."

The sun hadn't risen high into the sky when the sound of horse's hooves echoed from the courtyard. With a shout of glee, Gladra rushed to the window. Torsa had returned. She hurried to the strange man that had somehow touched her heart. "She is here with the rose," she caressed his face, searching for a sign that he would wake. "You will be well now."

Torsa laid her package on a dresser and pulled the edges of fabric away. "It lives. Look, Gladra."

In the dim light of the dingy room, the blood red rose drew her eye. "But he does not rouse."

"Lay it on his chest?" Torsa handed Gladra the flower. Gladra drew the blanket down and placed it on his bare skin. The deep color stood in stark contrast to his pallor, but he did not move.

"Try making a rose tea?" Torsa shrugged. "Will he drink?"

"He took water last night. We can try." Gladra carefully pulled two petals from the blooming rose. Their scent filled her nostrils. She went to the kitchen and lit one of the burners. She found an old cast iron tea pot, filled it with water, and set it in the fire. As steam rose from the opening, she placed the two petals into the pot.

"The flower fades, you must hurry." Torsa shouted as she grabbed the side of the doorway into the kitchen.

Gladra wasted no time. She removed the tea pot

and placed it on a tray with three heavy mugs. They would all drink. She held the tray steady as they returned to the sickroom. The rose had withered against his chest. She removed it and poured three cups of tea. The color of the petals had tinged the water, and the smell wafted sweet and strong.

She lifted his head slightly and dripped tea into his mouth. A red drop slithered down his chin and onto the blanket. She poured more into his mouth. He drank. Drip by drip, she emptied the mug. When at last she finished, she stared expectantly, but he lay still.

"Here," Torsa handed her a second mug. Gladra sipped at it, its flavor rich and sweet. "Not you," Torsa admonished, "him. What if he needs more?"

But the man on the floor began to stir. Gladra held the cup to Torsa. She gripped his hand once more. A smile burst out of her as his eyes fluttered open. His hand in hers squeezed back. She blinked against the foolish tears that wanted to fall. Dark and unfocused though they were, she remembered his eyes.

Deep groans shook the house and Gladra gripped his hand. He struggled to sit up. She put an arm around his shoulder, "Here, lean on me."

He held his hand up, turning it back and forth. Gladra couldn't imagine how it must seem to be human once again. Then he grabbed her around the waist, bounding to his feet with a joyous cry. Gladra squealed, wrapping her arms around his neck as he twirled them. She could see Torsa laughing, her hand covering her mouth. He kissed her, a sweet touch of lips against hers, and Gladra forgot about her sister.

Warm delight curled her toes even as embarrassment caused her to turn her head to the side.

Gladra blinked. She was back on the ground, world righted. Torsa pulled her away. "We should get cleaned up." She muttered something that sounded like nonsense. He was grinning, and Gladra felt butterflies invade her insides.

Torsa was still laughing as she pulled Gladra to the door. "My warrior sister tames the beast."

Gladra breathed easier as the stepped into the hallway and shut the door. "He is not a beast."

"Pretty close, all dark and sinewy." Torsa's eyebrows wiggled, and Gladra pushed her away with a laugh.

"Enough. I don't know what happened."

"I do. I believe it's called love." Torsa opened the door to the room she'd used. She tried to shut it just as quickly, but Gladra pushed through.

"What is this?" Throughout Torsa's bed chamber, boxes of treasures had been stacked. Gladra glared at her sister, but she received no response. "You were going to rob him? How could you? You know it is wrong to steal."

"I didn't know he was here. The stories were about a beast, an animal. And old, he shouldn't still live. I knew there would be—I mean, so much just waiting," she waved her arms weakly.

"You're not taking anything. You'll return it where it belongs." She stepped closer, her heart breaking at her sister's foolish greed. "How could you?"

"Father works hard, and there's three of us. How will we ever find good husbands? He can't afford to give us a season. We can't travel to any of those places we could meet eligible men. I just wanted to help." She hung her head. "I didn't think."

Gladra wrapped her arms around her little sister. What would he think of them? "We must tell him."

"I will take the blame."

"No. He cares for me. If he is angry, that will help." She took a step back and offered a wobbly smile. "Return these things." She left her sister. The day was still young, and even through the onslaught of emotions that had come throughout the morning, hunger gnawed. She returned to the kitchen.

The witch felt her heart thud even as she crossed the fields and entered the gate that should have been closed and locked. Age and death hovered just beyond her, eager to swoop in should she fail this final battle to regain her beast. She reached her hand out, nails latching onto the remnants of the curse, drawing what remained to herself. She prepared.

NINE

Breakfast was not her best effort. Gladra winced at the charred smell of ham that lingered around the iron stove. They wouldn't smell that in the dining area, would they? Slices of bread were a bit dark. Eggs mixed with ham, but both overdone. After carrying the platter to the table, she blushed when he stood to help, and his fingers brushed against her. She looked at him. He knew she felt something. Something inside her melted, coming alive. Something wonderful was making her want to grin like a fool and she had to bite the inside of her lip to keep from doing so.

"I'm starving." Torsa didn't seem to notice anything unusual and reached between them.

"Allow me." He served Torsa, giving her toast as well, which she gave a glance then raised a brow at Gladra. He next served Gladra and then himself.

The eggs had no flavor, but Gladra ate anyway to remove her eyes from him.

"I should share my story with you," he offered between bites.

"Not yet," Gladra sighed, laid her fork beside the plate, and began pulling at the tablecloth covering her lap. "We…I," she started again. "I must confess and beg your forgiveness."

"Forgiven."

She smiled at him. When had his face become dear to her? "It is not that easy. I intended to rob you."

He laughed. "Your sister, maybe."

Torsa blushed and lowered her face.

"You are forgiven as well." He spoke kindly to her, and Torsa lit up. He returned his attention to Gladra, and she suddenly felt as though she were twirling. "You came to defend her. I remember crossing blades with you. We'll have to do that again. You have talent."

"You don't understand." Gladra could remain seated no longer. She paced to the window. "We didn't come to help you. I mean, I wouldn't have hurt you, I just wanted Torsa home again. Safe, away from you."

"I understand. But am I as horrid as you thought? I was greedy enough to keep your sister here in hopes she would love me. I didn't care if she rummaged through the attics and the cellars, as long as she was willing to stay. Hope and despair plagued me day and night for she would have naught to do with me."

"Don't, please…" Gladra wanted him to stop.

"You were the first woman to stand up to me as though I were still a man. The swords didn't matter, you were magnificent."

"If you knew what Torsa did, why?"

"I don't care about her. She may take whatever she wants. Empty the manor, I will hire the coaches to return her to her home. If you will remain with me."

"As what?"

"Wife." He stood and stepped closer. "Confidant. Friend. Mother of our children." With each word he took a step closer. Gladra leaned against the wall.

"Am I interrupting something?" The flippant voice of her sister broke the trance. She closed her eyes thankfully.

"Yes." He growled but took a step back.

"I am not going to be able to leave the two of you alone, am I?" Torsa teased.

Gladra could feel her face flaming, but she sat and tried eating her eggs once more.

TEN

"Isn't this a cozy little scene."

Gladra felt a cramp in her stomach and her body stiffened unnaturally. Her lungs labored to keep air moving in and out as prickles spread across her skin. She heard Torsa moan beside her but could not turn her head to look.

"Stop this!" The man growled, hurling himself to his feet, unaffected by what had just entered the room.

"What happened to my lovely beast?"

A woman moved into view. An older woman with gray streaks in her black hair stood close enough to touch him, but he backed away.

"I am not yours. Your curse is broken, let the devil take you and be gone," he snarled.

"Had you but begged me to end it, I might have. One of these days I would have given in to you." She shook her head and glared, spilling hatred toward Gladra and Torsa. "But not like this, it cannot end this way."

Gladra felt something new stir within herself. Although she'd not led a life in fear, she'd never felt courage. This man had brought something to her life

133

that had been lacking, and something within herself woke to the knowledge this strange woman wasn't going to get to take him away from her.

The woman moved closer to Gladra and her sister. "I don't even remember what started it all." She waved her hands. "Someone wanted power over someone else. I was paid to place a curse on him, but not even I realized the benefits of tying my spell with a life force." She motioned and both sisters stood, still unable to do naught but what the witch required. She leaned between Gladra and Torsa, looking at him. "Do you realize the longer he lived, the longer I lived? And not just live, mind you, I stayed young." She held up her hands and moved them back and forth. "It stopped working, do you see the wrinkles?" She gave an ugly look at him. "Do you see what you've done to me?"

The witch's hand gripped the back of Gladra's neck, holding onto Torsa with the other. "Give me back my life, and I will spare theirs."

Gladra hurled herself from the wicked touch, kicking the strange woman away from them.

The woman rolled, then looked and screamed. "No! Not possible."

Gladra stood shaking, but she stood within her own power. "You had your life, now let him return to his."

The witch flew to her feet. "If this is to be my end, do you imagine I would let any of you live?"

"Gladra!" He pulled her to his side. She held onto the fabric of his shirt but refused to turn away.

"What a pretty picture you make." The witch scowled and waved her hand.

An Engling grew from a wisp of web on the floor. Gladra felt her heart skip a beat. Englings were nasty creatures from children's stories. Thin red hair dangled from their oval heads. They had dark beady eyes and bodies like small children, but wiry. If the tales were correct, a bite would send poison coursing through the body, death to follow. Gladra drew her sword, offering it to the man standing at her side.

But he shook his head, grabbing a knife from the table. "We do this together."

Gladra nodded, her body shaking but unwilling to give up easily. She grabbed a knife as well.

More creatures grew to join the first. Their chattering rose to a scream as they advanced. Gladra spun, pressing back-to-back with the man who was no longer a beast, using her sword to cut down any of the creatures that drew near enough. The elven blade sliced through the first one, deep burgundy blood smearing its silvery sheen. The creature lay dead on the floor. More rushed to take its place. The man pulled her away from blood spreading across the floor. One of the Englings had climbed onto a side table and another a nearby chair.

Rather than take flight, they fell inexplicably as a howling screech rushed through the room. He and Gladra spun as one to look. Torsa stood over the witch, the cast iron platter raised high in her arms, looking bewildered and sick. The witch lay crumpled at her feet.

Gladra gasped. "How?"

She lowered her arms but held the pan. "I was freed when you fought back. She paid me no heed and it was the only thing I could find to hit her with."

Gladra ran to her sister, helping her lay the platter on the table then taking her into her arms. He joined them, his hand warm on Gladra's back. They looked at the witch.

"What should we do with her?" Gladra wrapped an arm around his waist.

"The unbinding is taking its toll." He pointed at the witch's hair turning more and more gray. "We should leave Nimglen."

He did not need to urge them twice. They escaped through the front doors into a garden where roses were blooming once more. Torsa ran to the carriage, but he lifted Gladra and twirled with her in his arms, joy bursting from him. Gladra clung to him, laughing.

"I don't even know your Christian name." She pressed her hand against his heart.

"Tamor." He set her on the ground and covered her hand with his. "Tamor Nimglen." His eyes grew moist as he looked at her.

"Tamor." She repeated his name, and he kissed her. The beat of her heart matched his, but the kiss ended too quickly.

"Go to your sister," he whispered, his breath felt hot against her lips.

She pressed them against his cheek. "I love you." She whispered the words at his ear. The truth of it humbling and magical. She pulled away, but his hand lingered a moment at her waist. His eyes repeated her words back to her.

Sleeping Beauty's Potion
(Based on the fairytale Sleeping Beauty)

The origins of Sleeping Beauty come through German, French, and Norse traditions. Some of the earliest tellings are quite violent, including rape. The earliest renderings in print include the writings of Basile, Perrault, and the Grimm Brothers.

The telling here has a charming twist on the original. I'm sure you will enjoy reading as much as I enjoyed writing.

F lakes of snow drifted through the air, hanging suspended for a moment before falling to the hard earth. Rachel lifted her face, allowing the tiny crystals to sting her cheeks and melt into water. A hush settled across the glen, silent save for the sound of snow crunching beneath her feet. A few more steps, and the wall of roses stood before her. Even in the chill of winter, red blooms clung to thorny stems, thick leaves tipped with ice covered the twisted branches and brambles. For as long as she could remember, the hedge had stood, untouched, twisting thicker and higher.

She pulled the clippers from her pocket beneath her cloak as she made a selection. With her fingers curled beneath the flower, she cut the stem. One bloom once a year on the day her mother died. Using the clippers to strip the thorns, she then weaved the stem through her braid. Satisfied with her choice, Rachel skipped along the path that followed the hedge.

Snow made the dirt slick, and her foot slipped. With a gasp, she grabbed the bramble. Thorns sliced her hand as her feet flew out before her. She landed on her rump, with her stinging hand pressed into the wet snow. She bit her lip and wiped snow and blood across her brown jacket.

Cradling the injured hand against her chest, she wiped moisture from her eyes. Then paused. A section of the hedge seemed to have broken apart, providing a gap. She looked around, but no one else stood in the forest with her. She gathered her skirts and crouched beside the opening. She might just fit. She tugged her thick cloak as far down as it would go toward her fingertips, pulled the hood over her head. Gloves would be better, but she didn't want to waste time returning to the castle.

Rachel bent closer to the ground and crawled beneath the hedge. Roots knotted the ground, but it remained dry. The snow couldn't pass through the thick weave of branches and flowers. Something tugged at her back. She flattened herself against the ground and pushed forward. In a few moments, she cleared the hedge and slid into the hidden garden.

It wasn't snowing. Hadn't been snowing this side of the hedge. The sky overhead remained gray. Dead plants littered the garden and a stone path wound through, toward a massive house of similar color.

Rachel paused. Unlike the gentle hush of falling snow, this quiet held a hint of malice. Though the house resembled many found in the village, its curtains were tattered, and the back door was hanging on only one hinge. Nothing stirred. The upper windows were dark, looking like empty eyes staring down on her. She shivered. She should go back. This was not a place to play or wander. But what could be hidden inside? The roses had been there for an age, and no one ever spoke of a place hidden within. Were hers the first eyes to see?

She walked closer, stopping less than a stone's throw from the door. She tapped her foot. Her hand hurt, blood still seeping from the wound. At the least, she should find a cloth to bind it. With that thought, she moved onto the porch, pushed against the broken door, and stepped into the house.

The board beneath her foot creaked, and Rachel froze. Her heart pounded inside her chest. Nothing moved. There were no other sounds to be heard. The air smelled of old age. Windows provided enough light to see blanket-covered chairs, sofa, and a table. The hallway to the right led to the kitchens. The open back door revealed a vegetable garden filled with death. The ovens were cold and sink basin dry and rusting. She noticed nothing of interest, until she spied the stairs around a corner. Unremarkable in themselves, and yet, what may lie above? Someone had lived in the house. Could secrets be revealed in their bedrooms?

The house seemed to breathe with expectancy as she climbed. The steps turned and light dimmed. She slowed her pace as a long hallway came into view. The doors on either side were open, though most revealed nothing but darkness. All but one room. Toward the other end of the hallway, light spilled across the worn rug. Nothing moved, and still no sound. She crept closer, stopping before she stepped into the beam. She listened but heard nothing. Her hand ached. She should find something with which to bind it. But her feet refused to move backward. The need to know, to look for herself overwhelmed. She lifted one booted foot and broke through the beam of light. Nothing changed. She stepped forward. She stood close to the doorway. Just a peak. She leaned forward. The curtains over the windows on the far wall of the bedroom were pulled back, allowing light to fill the room. A bed with four posts was set against the side wall. Filmy white curtains were tied to the posts and draped between them.

Someone lay on the bed. Rachel could see their form through the curtain. She didn't remember moving, but somehow found herself standing beside the bed. She couldn't help it. She reached her hand out and pulled the curtain back.

Death lay upon the white covers. Rachel's hand stuck to the curtain even as a scream built in her throat. The silence of the house pressed in on her and she couldn't break it. Fear choked her. The figure on the bed looked young, and yet her cheeks had sunken. Her skin pulled across a skeleton. Light hair fanned out around her. She wore a white dress with a green sash, all that remained of her arms and hands crossing her chest was gray skin pulled tight against bones.

Rachel wanted to run, but her body remained frozen.

"Too long I have waited for this."

The voice came from behind. She tried to turn and look, but something else happened. Air moved around the bed, a wind that began to swirl. Rachel found her voice as the remains on the bed blew away like dust. She screamed, trying to hold the bedpost, but the wind was too strong. It pulled her forward, toward the center of the bed where the other had lain. Darkness opened before her. She scrambled to get away, but magic overruled her. She fell into darkness and knew no more.

~

"Jackson," Allister hollered, but the hound bounded through the snow. He gave chase. Across the field, he watched Jackson pause, lower his nose to the ground, and then jump between the trees. "Jackson." The dog did not appear. With a growl of his own, Allister crossed the field. Cold seeped through the leather of his hessian boots. There was enough other mutts to get a replacement. Teach the animal to come when called.

He followed the paw prints into the woods. He didn't care for the feel of branches overhead, the cluster of trees and brush on either side of the slim path Jackson seemed to be following. If his workers could see him now, they wouldn't recognize their stalwart boss. Cold dripped beneath his collar. Where had the dog run off to? He tried calling again, but the trees stood silent, not even bothering to direct his way. Then he heard the whimper. Something had been found by the mangy mutt. Allister broke into a jog. The trail took a sharp turn and he nearly landed in the tall wall of brush that appeared.

Not brush. Red roses, a deep color nearly black, grew over the wall. But it wasn't a wall built of stone. The rose bush itself had grown tall and thick enough to form a wall. He looked to the right and to the left. The wall of rose continued for some length. Jackson sniffed at a branch not far to his right. The dog lifted a leg and left a stream of yellow in the snow. Allister shook his head. Looking down, he noticed footsteps. Not just his dog's prints. Another dainty foot had made an impression in the snow. A human foot.

Someone else had been this way recently enough to still be visible in the freshly falling snow. He brushed at the accumulation of flakes on his shoulders. Bloody dog.

He followed the trail, stepping to the side. The smaller foot falls mingled with puppy paws meandered along the massive rose bush. It must belong to a woman with a light step. Jackson pounced across a patch where she had paused. And then she had run. He didn't find any traces of someone else. From what would she run? Or had it been for fun? Jackson stopped at another area. Mud showed through the snow, but there were also red splotches against the pristine white. Allister crouched.

He snapped his fingers at the dog panting beside him. "Jackson, sit." This time the dog obeyed, settling on its haunches at his side. The woman had been injured. He looked up. With the slick of mud, she must have slipped and grabbed onto the rose bush. Even from here he could see the wicked thorns tangled through the twisted branches and stems. A bit lower, he noticed the opening.

She couldn't be seriously injured, and he wasn't about to ruin more of his outfit. If the girl wanted to traipse through the bramble, so be it. He stood, but Jackson moved to the opening and turned to face him.

"No." The damn dog didn't obey. It disappeared beneath the rose bush.

Allister removed his jacket and laid it across a low branch. No point ruining everything he wore. The opening was not wide, but he managed to slip through without snagging his shoulders. The bush was not as wide as he had supposed, and he soon found himself nearing the other side. His shoulder stung, and he dropped to his belly with an oath. But it didn't stop. Something wrapped around his arm and tightened. He pulled against it, and then pain erupted. Instead of moving, he felt himself being dragged. Something else snaked around his other arm, more pain as thorns dug through his flesh. He cried out, struggling, making it worse, but he couldn't stop himself. A thorn tore across his cheek to his eyebrow as he was pulled from the thicket. Wet poured down his face. Agony washed through him as he was pressed against the bush. He gulped air in shallow bursts, fighting waves of darkness.

Something moved toward him. Someone. Flashes of light and dark danced before his eyes. The taste of blood filled his mouth as he tried to cry out. He spat. The bush held him tight. A woman stepped close enough he could feel her breath across his skin.

She gazed at him in silence until her hand moved toward him, but returned to her side before she touched him. "How did you get through?"

Her eyes were dark, slanted upward at the ends, giving her a foreign look. She seemed puzzled, and yet intrigued. Why did she not pull against the restraints to help free him?

"Who are you?" He sounded pale.

"I am the beauty that comes from death's sleep."

"Help me."

"Not I." She trailed a finger across his chest. White heat flared in its wake, and he hit his head against a thick branch. "None may enter, save those who will lay in my stead."

He gasped as the pain faded. "Who are you?"

"Do you believe in Faere Folk? Do their legends exist in the world as yet? When a child of the stars is borne, they will bring blessings to its chamber?"

"Are you one of the Faere folk?"

Her features darkened. "No. I am a child of the stars. I am one to whom they brought blessings. Or so they should have been."

"Hang a dream catcher in the windows to keep dark faeries from entering."

"Alas, my parents did not." She took a step back. "Am I not fair?" Her voice rose in a melody reminiscent of a songbird. "Is my voice not sweet?" She pressed her lips against his cheek. "Do I not smell sweet as honey on a midsummer breeze?"

His skin tingled with her touch, pain. "What curse did they bring you?"

Her lips thinned. "I was meant to sleep beginning on my eighteenth birthday. Until such a one as you," she waved her hand, "woke me."

She paced. Allister turned his head best he could. A vine from the rose bush had wrapped around his arm. With every movement, thorns pierced deeper into his skin. He closed his eyes.

"Mother wanted no such fate for me."

She had come closer, and he opened his eyes to find her a hands breadth away. "She found a way to curtail the curse. Circumvent its course, you might say. Such a price to pay."

"What price?"

"Have you noticed there are none to aid you? They were all taken, given over that I might be spared."

"Spared from sleep?"

Her eyebrows drew close. "Who knows what a Faere sleep entails? I may have been trapped for hundreds of years. Am I to wallow away my youth and beauty in such a way?" She shook her head. "It was not to be borne."

"So how have you broken the curse?"

"There is a potion. Others sleep in my stead. Time steals away their youth and beauty whilst I remain." She twirled.

"Remain here? Locked inside a gray world?"

Her lips pouted. "That would not be much of a life. I alone may pass through the wall and walk in the world. I live as I may until the beauty who sleeps for me has passed from this life." She snapped her fingers. "Or I make this world as I desire."

In an instant, the gray faded. Blue sky opened above them. The garden burst to life. Music poured from the house. People milled in senseless paths. The scene appeared vibrantly alive, and yet not real. As though it were a memory brought back.

"This isn't real, and you know it. Why else keep me here?"

"Are you that eager to meet death? It would not require much. All I have to do is pierce your neck with a thorn." She tilted her head, tapping a red painted fingernail against her lip.

~

Darkness weighed heavy, and yet something else pulled her. Something wet against her cheeks. Her forehead. Talons of sleep slipped away, and light pressed against her closed eyelids. Something warm rested across her chest, licking her face. With a grunt, she pushed herself up. The animal jumped from the bed. A dog? What was a dog doing in her chamber? She looked around. This wasn't her chamber. A white coverlet covered her. Curtains draped over the bed. Another body, drained of life, came to mind. With a cry of horror, Rachel jumped from the bed and staggered across the floor.

The dog barked, jumped against her, landing its two front paws on her thigh, and then pushing off to run across the room. It bounded over the bed and returned to her. A body had lain there, another girl. What had happened? Rachel shook her head. What was she doing?

Pain in her hand registered. She had come through the rose bush. But what had happened? She hadn't meant to fall asleep on the bed. Had intended to run, but something stopped her. Shivering, she raced from the room. The dog followed.

The house remained silent as she moved down the steps. Halfway through the kitchen, life broke out around her. Pans clattered. Fish simmered on the oven, flames sizzling. A large woman kneaded dough against a dirty cheese cloth. Rachel nearly jumped out of her skin. They weren't real. They were like ghosts. A small girl moved through her, and she didn't feel a thing. The back door remained open. She ran.

There were others outside. Gardeners pulling tomatoes from a plant that wasn't really there. A maid hung linen on the line between two trees. Rachel gulped against the sobs tightening her chest.

Through the blanket that waved in a breeze that

had yet to reach her, Rachel saw two others further away. A man and a woman who were thick like humans were meant to be, not visceral. She halted a few yards from them. Her throat clenched.

The man was not standing. He was wrapped in the hedge, tangled with it. Blood dripped down his sleeves and across his chest. The bottom part of his face was covered in it. The other was a woman, taller than Rachel. And cold, like an evil wind across the moors.

"All I have to do is pierce you neck with a thorn."

"No," Rachel cried out.

The other woman whipped around and paled. "How? What are you doing?"

"Release him." Rachel pointed at the hurting man. The other woman ignored her, but the stems seemed to move. He cried out.

The woman grabbed Rachel by the shoulders. "I need you to sleep."

Rachel struggled, trying to shake off the fingers digging into her shoulders. The woman grabbed her hair as she pulled a vial from a pocket. Rachel clawed at the arm. She hit the glass away. Something shattered on a brick paver. The woman stopped with a hiss.

"What have you done?"

Rachel pushed again, but the woman held firm and began to change. The hair at her temples paled, growing longer moment by moment. Rachel stared in horror. Smooth skin at the corner of her eyes pulled, forming crow's feet. Fear pounded in her, and Rachel struggled harder. She began screaming as the woman's face thinned.

Then strong arms were pulling her away, wrapping her against a warm chest. Air beat against her back, but with sobs escaping, she wrapped her arms around the man. He held her. She felt his cheek against her own. The battering stopped, and stillness settled around them once more.

She was shaking. Rachel didn't want to move, but he staggered. She tightened her arms around him and pulled back enough to look at him. Blood covered one side of his face. The white shirt he wore was soaked with it.

"Lean on me," she urged, keeping her arms around him.

"How did you break the curse?"

"What curse?"

"Beauty's curse. She used a sleeping potion to keep others in her own fate. She said it would take a kiss to end it."

"A kiss?" Rachel blushed. Had this man kissed her? "Did you make it to the house?"

He shook his head. "I was trapped in the rose bush."

"Then how?" A dog barked, running a circle around them. Rachel raised her brows as she looked at the excited animal. "The dog? I remember now, he was licking my face when I woke."

The man laughed, then groaned in pain. "Jackson. He loves people. The Faere must not have spoken what type of male must be used to break the spell."

"Rescued by a mutt?" She shifted so they faced the wall of roses. How were they to get through?

"He is a fine hound. He found you, your trail in the woods, that is. Must have known you were trouble."

"What?"

"In trouble." He laughed and winced with more pain.

She meant to respond, but the thick hedge of roses surrounding the house moved. Branches thicker than her wrist jerked as though something large and strong beat on them. With a screech, the hedge of roses tumbled into the earth. The hedge thinned until the wall had broken down to one remaining section. Jackson barked but remained at their side.

The man clung to her shoulders and shivered. "I am ready to leave this place."

"My home should not be far. We can tend to your wounds."

Flakes of snow began to fall around them. It was a strange world through which they moved. Snow fluttered through the air. The cloud-covered afternoon was brighter than the gray of the house. Had it been a house? With each step, Rachel became more and more uncertain of the events that had occurred. By the time they reached the castle at the edge of the village, she knew she had found the injured man, but how his injuries had been sustained, she could not say. Loss of blood had taken its toll. Though he moved his legs step by step as she pulled him along, his body felt cold, and he leaned more heavily.

"Gail, Martin, your help," she hollered as they drew within hearing distance. Familiar servants ran toward her. The older gentleman, Martin, grabbed the stranger before he could fall to the ground.

"What trouble have you found yourself today, little miss?"

She shook her head. "I do not know."

"Tisk." Gail pulled her away. "He's half alive. And what of you?"

"I am well, he needs help. Get him settled, a downstairs room, I think. I will fetch the doctor."

~

Pain stabbed his arm as he moved. With a groan, Allister shifted to consciousness. He hurt. His cheek throbbed. His arms pounded. What the blazes happened? Something cool touched his forehead.

"Sh."

He turned his head toward the soft voice. "At least my nurse is a pretty thing."

She frowned. "Don't fun, or I'll slap your arm."

"Please, no. they hurt as it is."

"Serves you right, getting tangled like that."

Like what? His mind had grown foggy. What had tangled him? Where?

A puzzled look crossed her face. She wasn't certain either. "It wasn't pleasant, whatever it was."

"Neither one of you remember, do you?" A woman stood inside the door to the room. Tall, with thick dark hair falling like a curtain, she wore a burgundy dress with a high collar. An underskirt of black peeked through. Something about her set him on edge. He pushed his elbows, ignoring the white-hot flare of pain, as he struggled to rise.

"Be still, boy." She waved her hand.

The young nurse pressed against his chest. Her

touch was cool, unlike another's that had been like an iron.

"Move too much you will rip open the stiches. Doc worked hard patching you together." The woman smiled, though it did not warm her eyes.

"Do you know him?" The nurse looked from him to the woman.

"No." They spoke together. Allister leaned back. He clenched his fists and released. The motion hurt, but he did it again. Small steps to rebuilding his strength.

She smiled again, and the glint in her eyes put him on edge. "No, indeed. But something this important I had to see for myself." She moved closer to the bed.

The nurse took his hand.

The strange woman ignored her and leaned closer to him. "How did you break the spell? I sense nothing remarkable about you."

"Because it wasn't him."

Another woman entered the room. Older, gentler features with hair pulled into a loose bun and gray gown. He felt the nurse stiffen.

"Grandmother."

"Rachel, dear. I am pleased to see you well. Your young man looks more battered."

He squeezed her hand. Rachel. The name suited her.

The other woman huffed. "Your Goddaughter?"

"Granddaughter, actually. Turn your head, dear. Show Priscilla what you've tucked in your hair."

Rachel acquiesced. He looked. She wore a rose, its vibrant red standing out against her tawny hair.

"That is not…" Priscilla stammered.

"It is." The grandmother looked pleased. "Faere blood runs within her."

Priscilla shook her head. "Had she gone through the bush, Beauty would have used the potion. Her last victim had been sucked dry. She needed fresh youth."

"The sleep of death." He'd heard those words.

Priscilla whipped around. "You were there?"

"It matters not." The grandmother stepped between them. "The curse is broken, Beauty is destroyed. The hedge is all but gone. Now you must go."

Anger twisted Priscilla's face. "It won't last. Their first child, I'll find a way."

"Go. You've darkened the house long enough."

With a growl of frustration, Priscilla stomped from the room.

The grandmother walked to Rachel and patted her cheek. "That woman never could stand to lose. I don't know how you did it, but you did good." She turned to him. "And you, young man. You as well. A handsome man you are, with a bit more heart than you thought you had." Her eyes twinkled.

"Grandmother," Rachel blushed.

"Yes, well. All in good time. He must heal first." She kissed Rachel's head, patted his foot, and took her leave.

Quiet settled the room and he realized he still held her hand. He liked the feel of it. From the soft smile on her lips, she didn't seem to mind either.

The Frog Curse
(Based on the fairytale The Frog Prince)

The origins of the Frog Prince go back to the thirteenth century, in Germany. It did not always involve a kiss, though the Brothers Grimm wrote that in their version as a revision on the earlier story where a violent act resulted in breaking the spell.

The idea of kissing a frog is repugnant, and yet, metaphorically speaking, I think we've all kissed a few. Ponder that, as you enjoy this retelling.

Chapter 1

Catherine Le Guin stiffened her shoulders as her young suiter stood with his hat in his hands. The velveted rim would never be the same. But that wasn't where her attention should be. "I am sorry," he said, staring at the ground. "Meeting Anastasia changed everything."

Catherine blinked. "You told me your intentions at the start of the season. I never considered any other beau."

He twisted the hapless hat some more. "I hope you will forgive me."

Catherine drew in a shuddering breath. "Of course." The words came even though she wanted to beat on him. The heart wants what the heart wants. Which, in Coleman's case, was someone with a larger purse.

She watched him leave, then caught a glimpse of herself in the long, gilded mirror hanging from the picture rail. Her curls fell from ivory hair combs in preparation for the evening's dance. Her pale face made her gray eyes darker. She grimaced at her reflection. No point strapping herself into the gown prepared for tonight's entertainment.

She hurried back to her bedroom, flinging herself across the fourposter bed draped in lilac brocade. Tears she expected to flow did not. There was a tightness to her throat, and an ache in her chest. Perhaps an uneasy feel in her stomach region. And a blister on her right heel… she flopped over to stare at the canopy above the bed. Flowers danced across the fabric. She blinked. Even in early fall, the gardens had flowers and greenery to design bouquets. It was what her bedroom needed.

Her mind paused only a moment on what might have been. With a sigh, she put on the brown apron she used to protect her clothes from getting dirty in the garden.

~

"Kiss me."

Catherine jumped, but no one stood in the garden save herself. Odd thing to hear, to think. "That batty Anastasia steps out with your suitor, and you start hearing things among the flowers." Catherine muttered, digging her toe beneath a wilting dandelion.

"You are not alone, I am here." The voice ended with a gurgling croak.

Catherine held her breath. She heard something. Definitely, heard something. She twisted slowly, yet no one stood behind her. "What manner of joke is this?" She stomped her foot. Someone was playing games.

"No joke, dear lady. I have not laughed in ever so long. Years. Decades perhaps." The short speech ended in another croak.

Catherine followed the sound of the voice until

she looked at the ground. A massive frog sat among the reeds of the pond a few steps in front of her.

"See, I am here. And I did request a kiss."

Catherine screamed. She scurried back, but the damp leaves offered no traction for her shoes, and she fell on her bottom. The thing leapt forward, landing a few feet from her. Her throat clogged and her eyes blurred with tears. "I am mad. My broken heart has been driven over the edge." She hadn't loved Coleman that much, had she?

The frog's face took on the human look of exasperation. "You are not mad. I am an unfortunate prince trapped in this ridiculous form."

"A what?" Her voice caught. She swallowed, closed her eyes, and counted to three. She peaked, but he remained, a lump of green. She cleared her throat. "A prince?"

"Yes, a prince, hard as that may be to comprehend. Bewitched prince, but royal none the less. Prince Adderbatt."

"Adder-" She shook her head. "That is not a name with whom I am familiar."

The creature sighed. "I do not know if my kingdom still stands. How long have I been locked by this enchantment?"

"Who? Why would they do such a horrible deed?"

It hopped closer. "A witch." He lowered his head. "I deserved something, I suppose, for toying with her. She was young and beautiful and I a spoiled prince."

Catherine tucked her feet beneath her as it inched a smidge closer.

"I did not realize who she was." Prince Adderbatt continued. "I wanted to dance, to steal kisses. I wanted to know passion before I was to wed the woman chosen by my father."

Catherine frowned. "You toyed with her while you were engaged to another?"

The frog flopped on the ground. "Years, many years I have had to contemplate the errors of my way. I would beg her forgiveness if I could, but I do not know where to find her."

"Witch's curses can be broken." She tried to scoot further away.

"That is my dilemma. As the lowest of servants, I may have had a chance. But this? In the body of a slimy frog? What fool would kiss me?"

"Not fall in love, just kiss?" Her stomach turned at the thought of pressing her lips against the moist skin of a frog.

"The witch said a kiss. Not even my own mother would give me time to explain. She beat me with a broom and forced me to leave the castle."

The story was ridiculous. She should run. The thing would never catch up, never find her again. But his eyes were sad. His mouth turned down, as if knowing she longed to flee. Her chest warmed. The poor thing… prince… trapped so long. "What if it has been too long? What if breaking the spell now results in old age, or death?"

The creature sighed. "I would much rather die a man than live as this forsaken creature. The beasts know I am not as I appear. Humans turn from me in disgust. There has been no companion, no friend." Something blinked over his eyes as he gulped, throat bulging slightly. "She left me utterly alone in her bitterness."

"You are a pitiful creature. I wish our paths had not crossed this day." Before she could lose her nerve, or talk herself out of it, Catherine leaned forward and kissed the oversized frog on the top of its head.

The green creature stared at her with eyes turning blue. "You kissed me." He seemed surprised.

Odd. The air around them wavered and broiled.

The skin across his face pulled and paled. The frog truly was human. He, a prince.

For a moment, Catherine basked in her action. She saved him. Her lips tingled. Or was it her face? Indeed, her whole body tingled like someone scraped a fork across her skin. "What's happening?" There was something strange with her arm. It looked long and thin, stretching out, turning a horrid shade of green, like early grass.

"Sorry love. You should have run. Bad luck, meeting here today and listening to my story." He had grown quite a bit, or was she that much smaller? His lips pressed into a frown. "You did it from the goodness of your heart. No filling you with ale, spinning tales of romance, or offering huge sums of recompense."

She croaked, an odd deep sound that rattled through her chest. Horror shook her. She croaked like a frog.

"You'll get your voice, you will." He reassured her with a pat to her head. "Took me a bit of time to adjust." He stood, stretched his hands above his head, and pushed up onto the balls of his feet. "Oh, that feels marvelous." He had become a fully human man wearing britches, a white shirt with lace cuffs and a fancy collar covered by a crimson jerkin with a row of golden buttons.

"Why am I…" Her words rolled through a garbled gurgle. The skin at her throat pushed out.

He clapped his hands. "Quick learner. Your parents must be proud. Now what did you ask? Why?"

She nodded. He twisted his upper body to the left and then to the right. Bent at the waist. "Why. Right. You would want to know that. Seems this curse has been in play for quite some time. I met a man with a talking frog. Can you imagine? A talking frog?" He shrugged and grinned. "I guess maybe you can." He rubbed his chin. "Hm, we shared a few drinks. I got a bit carried away and kissed myself a frog. I'm sure she'd have kissed me properly when the spell broke. But I was the frog and she'd already made that mistake."

Catherine's mind whirled. Her body felt the way it should, only scrunched, trapped in a tiny box. How had she gone from wallowing in misery over Coleman's betrayal to being bewitched in the body of a frog? "You knew this would happen?"

"Don't cry, love. I'm only a man after all. You're a pretty little thing. Won't take you long to convince another to give you a peck."

"How could you? What harm have I done you?"

"None. This was never about revenge. At first, with the original prince perhaps, but since then, it's about getting out and moving on."

"I could never do this to another. There must be

a different way to break the curse."

"Leave it for another," he scoffed. "Take care of you for now, like I took care of me. Let a different bloke figure it out."

"You have to help me."

"I would, really, I think I would." He scrunched his brows. "Kind as you are, but I've been trapped ever so long. I want to stretch my legs. Find home. Recover what I lost."

Sobs turned to froggish noises. "You can't leave me like this, not alone. Take me where you met the others. Help me find them."

Prince Adderbatt frowned, arms crossing his chest. His chin stuck out a bit. "It's not fair, you ask too much."

"I am not. Think how you felt at first. Didn't you want someone to help you?"

The man ran his hands through his hair. "I suppose I'd be heading that direction on my own. Might as well carry you with me. I'll even help you find a nice lad. Get past this and we can go our separate ways."

He caught her around the middle. Catherine flapped arms and legs. She was falling.

"Take it easy, lady. I'll find a box or something to carry you. Settle down."

She closed her eyes and scrunched her body as tight as she could.

Chapter 2

It took the better part of an evening for Prince Adderbatt to find a basket for her. He added a layer of grass pulled from a nearby field before plopping her into it. Her gasp caused him to frown as he lifted the basket with her in it. "This is deuced uncomfortable. I need a wagon to pull you."

"How big am I?" Catherine couldn't figure it out. Everything felt tight and squished.

"Took both hands to hold you, not touching."

She shuddered at the thought. The basket swayed, causing her head to spin. "Will you walk all night?"

"I am too excited not to keep going." He said as he gave the basket a little wiggle. "I have no idea how long it has been since I stretched my legs."

Catherine wanted nothing more than to stretch her own, but she could not. She curled up and tried to sleep despite constant shifting, tilting, and swaying.

~

"Look at this," Prince Adderbatt declared, causing Catherine to gurgle as he dropped the basket on something.

She'd been dreaming about a lovely ball and twirling with a crowd of dancers. It was odd. She'd never been to an assembly so crowded, nor seen gowns with ridiculously wide skirts. "Where are we?" She peered over the top of the basket. Her froggish eyes noticed a fly crawling on the wall. Everything else seemed gray.

"I finally stopped. We are at an inn in Walingford."

"Does that mean we are close to your destination?"

He shrugged as he pulled off his jacket. "I am unfamiliar with this road. We shall enquire about directions."

She slid back into the basket. How long was she doomed to this fate?

The door latch unhooked. Catherine pushed herself high enough to see. "Prince Adderbatt, where are you going?" He stood in the open doorway. Thoughts of being alone with herself scared her.

He grinned. "Call me Andy. I cannot ask directions if I remain here."

She gulped. "You will come back?"

"Of course. You worry too much." His grin widened.

Catherine didn't trust him, but what choice did she have?"

~

Dreams washed through her in the dark of night. A woman with green eyes watched a tall man dance with another woman. She followed their progress as the light in her gaze dimmed to bleakness. Catherine wanted to cry, but frogs didn't do things like that.

The scene faded. The tall man accepted a drink from a boy as the woman with the green eyes watched from a distance. Pain etched the tall man's face.

She wanted to turn away or wake up in her own room. Catherine did neither. The man fell to his knees. Though he cried mercy, the woman crouched beside him and laughed. In another moment, she lifted a massive frog in her arms and twirled around the room with him. Then Catherine was being twirled, cold hands keeping her captive. The cry that rose in her throat couldn't be heard, but it didn't keep her from screaming.

Sunlight streaked across the basket, and she awoke with a loud croak.

"None of that," Andy growled, striking the side of the basket.

Another croak escaped as she wobbled. "What's wrong with you?"

He rubbed his head. "Nothing. I'd forgotten the aftereffects of too much ale."

"What are we going to do today?"

He winced. "Aren't you full of questions this morning. I'm going to eat breakfast."

"I'm hungry." She felt hollow.

"I've been told they have a salted ham with eggs that is decent."

Normally, she would have enjoyed such a breakfast, but her froggy body didn't seem interested. "I have no teeth. How would I eat such things?" Light from the window blazed. "What did you eat?"

He was silent a moment then tilted his head. "My memories of that experience fade. Perhaps I should put you in the garden and let you decide what will suit."

"No, I do not want to go outdoors." She rushed her protest. "Bring me something." She scrunched her body. "I feel safer here, with you." She wasn't completely truthful, but she knew he would most likely leave her in the garden, going on without her, if he could.

He chuckled. "Can't take you to breakfast, luv, not like this. Should I find you a lad? Fastest way to clear you out of this mess."

"By putting someone else into it? No thank you." She warbled, her throat billowing out. "We return to the place where you were cursed."

Andy sighed. "If you insist, although I don't understand why you can't end things now."

He left the room before she could respond. She hopped from the basket onto the table. The window didn't seem too far. Her sense of distance proved false, and she landed on the floor. The rag rug scratched at her soft belly. She grunted. Then her eyes caught a scuttle of something tiny in a corner past the bed. She went after it without thinking.

Finding nothing else of substance, she plopped on the wood floor to wait. Andy returned sooner than she expected.

"Trying out your legs? What a good girl you are." He sounded jovial. He dumped something in the basket, grabbed her, and put her there as well. "Found something you should enjoy. You can search it out while we travel."

She had the sinking suspicion he meant to leave the premises without payment. She pawed through the lettuce as he wrangled the basket with other supplies. As long as he took her with him, what could she do?

LAURIE LEE

Chapter 3

Catherine folded her legs beneath her and leaned over until her head rested against her arms. Days of travel, and now this, stuck in a dinky room on a narrow bed that smelled peculiar, even to her froggish nose, while Andy spent his time in the main room of the pub. Though he provided greens crawling with creatures and a bowl of water, how long had it been since they'd arrive? This wasn't where he'd met the others, and though she'd pleaded, he wasn't ready to move on.

The door burst open, swinging against the wall, and back again, hitting Andy in the head. Though the abrupt noise startled her, she couldn't stop a giggle.

"That's a good girl, keeping your spirits up." He rubbed his head with one hand and grabbed the basket with his other.

"Are you ready to leave?" Catherine glanced at the dark window. "Maybe we should wait for morning."

"You've been here too long, my girl. Soon you'll be thinking froggy thoughts and forget you were ever a lovely young lady."

He scooped her up with one hand and dropped

her into the basket.

"What are you doing?"

"Winning a bet, love. I have use of gold coin."

"A bet about me? But we decided it was better for me to remain a secret." She crawled across the bottom of the basket, causing it to wobble.

He slapped the side. "Be still. This is a better idea. I told you spending a few days among these clever folks would be to our benefit."

"Yours, not mine." She croaked.

"Tisk. What benefits me benefits you. We are happily tangled together. And there are gents for your choice. Big ones, small ones, smart ones, tall ones. Ale and your tears should convince the hardest of them to give you a kiss."

She heard the door slam. He was none too careful taking the stairs, rocking the basket this way and that, until Catherine flattened herself against the bottom and prayed it would be over soon. With a jolt, the basket came to rest on a table. Shadowy figures moved above her, but Catherine remained still.

"Blimy, that's a huge beast."

"Devil of the swamps, I'd say."

Something poked her. "Is it alive? You claimed it could talk. Said nothin' bout a dead frog."

"She's not dead. Not yet. Frightened, most likely. Give her a bit of room. Let me get her out of this thing."

With no other warning, the basket tilted over, and Catherine rolled onto the table. She gasped, hopped. There was nowhere to run. Nothing under which she could hide. Her body shook as she huddled.

"Look at those eyes. Mayhap she can speak."

Andy grinned. "Give her a kiss, she'll speak for you."

"No." Catherine glared at him.

One of the men straightened. "Odd noise for a frog. Sounded like a word."

Andy grinned. "You don't want a kiss?"

"Ask what happens, if he'll tell the truth." Catherine backed away from the hand reaching toward her.

"Those were words." Others around the table gasped.

"You heard her." Andy gleamed. "You all heard, she spoke, as I said she would. I'll take your coin."

Catherine simmered. "You win, now return me to the room. I don't like it here."

The others burst into laughter, but Andy pushed her into the basket. She struggled on her back, trying to right herself.

"Wait." A stranger's voice halted the revelry. "Let me see this creature."

Someone righted her. In the dim light of the pub, she couldn't see much more than the hand of the man tilting the basket toward himself.

"What happens if I give her a kiss?"

"No," Catherine hissed.

"Breaks the curse, of course." Andy hushed her with his hand.

She shook him off. "No, it doesn't. It passes it to another."

"Looks like your pet doesn't wish to play the same as you, sir."

"She'll find herself in the dirt, on her own after this," Andy growled.

The stranger smiled, rubbing his chin. "Let me take her off your hands. You've the look of a man who'd rather not be saddled with responsibility."

"He cannot." Catherine turned to Andy. "You promised to take me."

Andy shrugged. "He's as good a man as any I've seen."

"You don't know that," Catherine pleaded, but the stranger had his hand across the basket and lifted her from the table.

Andy raised his mug, offering a salute, and then he was gone. The cool evening breeze swept across her back.

Chapter 4

Catherine hunched inside the basket, pulling her arms closer to her body. "You got a smaller basket."

The stranger had said nothing the previous night, though he'd moved her to a different inn. He'd given her a second bed, arranging the covers in the middle allowing her sleep without falling.

As though she could sleep. How could she find the others who knew about the spell?

"It's the same basket."

"Is not." She gurgled. "It's smaller."

"I've been to breakfast and carried nothing with me in return. When could I have bought a smaller basket?"

"I'm pressed against the sides."

"You're bigger." He grunted as he lifted her. "And heavier."

Catherine pouted. Liar. "You did something."

"I would have if I could. I even offered to kiss you."

"Why did you take me from Andy… Prince Adderbatt?"

He laughed. "That man is not a prince. He would have dumped you in the field and been rid of you."

It was true, but the stranger wore on her nerves, and she wanted nothing to do with him.

He was tall and slender with a scruffy face. The frog eyes distorted color, making his skin sallow. A design in dark swirls twisted across his wrist. She peeked over the side. "What's that?" she pointed with her arm, then drew her arm back, hiding it beneath her body. She'd seen wrong. She wiggled it against her belly. Drummed her fingers. They felt like fingers, not the webbed toes to which she'd become accustomed. She drew her arm out again. Still green, but more like the arm of a girl, not a frog. She croaked and pulled it back under her body.

"What is it?" The stranger looked at her.

She gulped. Blinked back tears. "Nothing."

"Then why are you crying?" He sighed. "We'll get a larger basket."

"That's not it." She rolled to her side so he could see.

He set her on the ground and crouched beside her. He touched her human-looking hand, and she gripped her fingers around his.

"What's happening to me?"

"I don't know. Can you feel that?" He rubbed against her arm.

She nodded.

"What did Andy look like when you first saw

175

him?"

"Like a frog. The way I look. Looked." Why was she crying? She should be glad.

"You don't look like a frog. You didn't last night and even less so now."

"I don't understand."

"Why did you want to remain with Andy?"

"He promised to take me to the ones who had the curse before him. I need to find the witch whose broken heart created the curse to start with."

"Broken heart? I doubt there will be any truth to that. She knew precisely the sort of man he was and what he'd do to be rid of the curse."

He straightened, and with a gasp, Catherine felt herself lifted into the air once more. She harrumphed. The man hadn't even bothered to tell her his name yet.

~

"Why are we stopping?" Catherine shook herself from sleep.

"There's someone I want to speak with."

She wrinkled her nose. "It smells weird."

The dim hallway with its worn red carpet did not feel safe. The room into which he carried her had webs swaying from the ceiling in a breeze coming through the cracked window. He didn't bother with a bed but placed her on the dresser.

"No need to worry. We shan't be here long."

"This place has an evil feel." She flattened herself in the bottom of the basket.

He lit a candle. "It's not a place you'd come on your own, but I have a purpose here. Once I finish, we leave."

Not that he gave her a choice, leaving her on the dresser and locking the door three times. She slept, until he returned. Hopefully it was he who twisted the locks and pushed through the door. Dusk left little glow coming through the windows and the candle had gone out.

"Here we are. Let me light another candle." His voice boomed into the room, as though to relieve her of any doubts.

"Oh my, your friend has a powerful spell upon her." The second voice was that of a woman of an older age. Catherine peeked over the edge as he lit the candle on the desk. An older woman looked at her with eyes of steel. Her gray hair was tied in a neat bun at the back of her neck. Her clothes were ordinary traveling clothes. What she could see of her shoes looked to be serviceable. But those eyes... Catherine wanted to hide from them. She wrapped her arms around herself and huddled beneath the thin cover.

He swept it off anyway, exposing her.

Catherine glared at them both. "Who are you?"

The woman cackled. "Mrs. Glarse will do. I admire a girl with spirit."

He rolled his eyes. "What about the spell?"

"It is an old spell. A hundred years or more, I'd say." Mrs. Glarse pulled on Catherine's arm and turned her hand over. "An unravelling spell. The weaver of this spell will be most distraught."

"But if it is that old, how do we know she yet lives?" Catherine perked up.

Mrs. Glarse released her. "It is the nature of the weave. The witch bought herself long life with a perpetuating spell. As long as this frog curse is passed from one victim to the next, she has succeeded. But you are managing to break it."

Catherine rubbed her hands together, hope flickering to life within her heart. "That is a good thing." The skin above her eyes puckered.

"A good thing?" Mrs. Glarse chortled. "Only if you manage to keep the witch from finding you until the spell has been completely unwound."

"Why?" Catherine shrunk at the old woman's ominous tone.

Mrs. Glarse peered at the man. "You managed an innocent, didn't you, Rorry." She returned her steel gaze on Catherine. "My dear girl, you are costing the weaver of this spell her life. As more and more of the threads that bind you break, the witch feels her power drain away. She must find and destroy you before the spell is completely undone."

Catherine looked at Rorry. That couldn't be true.

His lips thinned. "It is as I feared. She should have passed the spell when she had the chance."

"Not possible now." Mrs. Glarse sat on the edge of the grimy bed. "The spell is breaking. It cannot be passed. What is your name, girl?"

"Catherine," she grunted.

Mrs. Glarse nodded. "Catherine. Your goodness has been your downfall."

"No." Catherine shivered with fear, but a stronger sense of strength offered courage. "The one who made me good will provide what I need to win this battle." She gulped. "He must. I don't want to die."

The old woman shook her head. "Believe that if you wish. You can expect a battle indeed. Even with a champion such as this," she jerked her thumb at Rorry, "don't expect much success." She harrumphed, slapped her knees with her hands, and pulled herself to her feet. "A pleasure, Rorry. I look forward to hearing the outcome. If I should meet another little talking toad, I will know success has not been met."

They crossed the room and walked through the door but left it open.

"Leave her as soon as you can. What were you thinking, taking up with her in the first place?"

"The idiot she was with would have dumped her in the swamps. She'd be dead." Rorry replied.

"Hers is a death sentence no matter what. Her innocence attracts you. You should not have allowed it to sway you." There was a pause, and then the old woman continued. "You think you know the spell weaver."

"And it is long past time for our reunion."

"Be careful, Rorry."

No more was said. Catherine hunkered down as he reentered the room and closed the door. Why did he want to be reunited with the witch? Did he mean to help her or deliver her to the enemy?

"What now?" Catherine watched as he crossed the room, blowing out the candle on the desk, then the one beside her on the dresser. He stood at the window, watching night settle across the land.

"What do we do now, Rorry, if that is indeed your name?" He was silent and moody, not her type.

"We won't stay here. This isn't a good place for

you."

"You think the witch will come?"

"How could she not? She will not be far. Look at how much you have changed."

Indeed, Catherine could now make out her legs as well as arms. She had feet and hands. Her skin remained green, no hair on her head. She gripped the edge of the blanket, felt better with it wrapped around her.

Rorry rubbed a hand through his hair. "Yet a few days and you will be released from this nightmare."

"Unless she finds me first?" Catherine gulped.

"I will keep watch."

Chapter 5

B ut on the first night, she woke to find him sleeping in the chair, head against the side rail, mouth hanging open. "Some watchmen you make," she grumbled, her voice croaking.

He straightened. "What?" His eyes looked weary, rimmed with red, as though he had passed most of the night watching for the shadows.

"Nothing." Shame caused her to lower her eyes. She heard him stretch, strange sounds emanating from his mouth.

"I could use a break from the fast of night. What of you, my green friend?"

"I am not--" she closed her mouth. He was teasing her.

"Not what, green?" He grinned. He took her by the chin and tilted her face. "No, still green, though a bit more flesh colored."

Catherine opened and closed her mouth at least three times. He left the room, but still, she could find no retort to satisfy the ache in her chest.

~

They traveled that day, him on the cushioned seat of a carriage while she rocked at his feet. She hid beneath the cover, but her body felt freer, as though the box in which she'd been trapped had grown. Maybe they could do it, continue moving and keep ahead of the witch. The carriage rumbled. Catherine pressed her hands against the larger basket to steady herself.

They stopped. Mutterings and grumblings she couldn't understand, and then he picked up her basket. "Lay down, before anyone sees you." Rorry pushed her head and threw a second blanket across the top of the basket. She heard him grunt as he lifted the basket. Lugging it from side to side as he walked made her stomach nauseous. They entered a room. He dropped the basket beside the door, not bothering to carry her to the bed.

"What are you doing?" She peaked from beneath the cover.

He frowned at her. "Going to find you something to wear." With that, he closed the door and left her in another strange room, still in the basket on the floor.

She used a choice word and sat up. Something changed. She looked down. The froggish body had a more human shape to it. She had legs, feet, and toes, although webbing still hooked her toes to each other. She had arms and a torso. She wrapped the blanket around her naked body. Her skin was still green, her body more child-sized than adult. She touched her head. Rather than smooth amphibian skin she felt short wisps of hair. Joy leapt through her. "The curse is almost gone."

The door opened and closed. "But we are stuck." Rorry tossed her a girl's dress. She managed to get it over her head with the blanket in place.

She wrapped the blanket around herself, feeling a chill in the air. "What do you mean, stuck?"

"I cannot travel with a green companion. Having to stay means the witch will find you all the faster."

"I will keep myself wrapped in the blanket. No one will see."

"You don't think they'll notice you growing bigger? Travelers in this region are more likely to kill an oddity before asking questions." Rorry shook his head. "No, further travel is not safe."

"So that's it? You'll leave me here and let the witch find me? You told that old woman it was long since time for a reunion. Is that what I am? Bait?"

He gave an exasperated sigh. "I'm hungry. Do you want real food or more bugs in your lettuce?"

"I'll go on my own." She stood, arms crossed, looking up at him, feeling like a young child threatening to run away.

He looked at her. "You are safer with me, and you know it. What do you want for dinner?"

She was hungry for real food, no longer drawn to froggy snacks lingering in the corners of the room. She shivered. "I'll try some stew, and maybe a pint of ale."

"Stay here. I'll bring it back to the room."

He left, and Catherine fumed. What right did he have to boss her around? She looked at the window. Night had settled. She pulled on the sash and heaved, the effort making her a bit dizzy. Fresh air caused the white curtains to wave. She dowsed the candle's light and returned to the window. They were on the upper floor, but a dormer brought the roof lower to the ground. A manageable jump, she surmised. "Especially for one who's been a frog these many days." The sound of her voice surprised her. There was no croaking or gulping. She gave a glance at the door which remained shut.

Rorry was right. Staying in one place wasn't safe for her. Leaving was her best choice, and if he refused to continue to travel with her, so be it. She would travel on her own. She pulled herself onto the bed and walked to the side table that sat in front of the window. She stepped onto it, crouching to take one last look at the door. Part of her wanted it to open, for him to keep her from leaving on her own. But what if his interest wasn't to her benefit? If this experience taught her anything, it was foolish to trust those she didn't really know. She crawled through the window.

Chapter 6

Leaving had been foolish. How soon could she turn around and not give him a victory? Crickets chirped as she crossed from the mud-thickened road to a grassy knoll leading to a small pond. Shadowed trees lingered across the glen, their branches swaying in a gentle breeze. The air held the warm musk of a summer's eve. Catherine pulled the blanket closer. Dampness clung to her skin. Was she still green?

There was a clatter of hooves in the distance, but Catherine remained off the road. The cicadas began their evening performance. Darkness had settled.

"What have we here?"

Catherine whirled around at the scraggly voice. Someone approached. Not Rorry with his quiet strength, but a woman that made her insides shiver.

"Taking an evening stroll this close to the swamps? Do you enjoy the feel of mud oozing through your toes?" She stepped closer.

Catherine shook her head but could not find her voice to reply.

"Are you her, my little frog princess? Are you the trouble that haunts my dreams?"

"Your trouble?" Something flared to life within her. The quiet reserve melted away and she wanted to stomp her foot. "I spent my eighteenth birthday as a frog."

"Funny thing, curses." The witch took a step closer. "They do go on. Who would have thought someone would have kissed that little--" The woman took a breath. "Kiss him she did, and my perfect little revenge took an unexpected twist."

"You shouldn't have done it anyway. Just because a man is rot…"

"What do you know about it?" The witch pressed close. Catherine stumbled away, but the old woman grabbed the front of the dress that had grown shorter and tighter than Catherine liked. "Look at you, a curse unbound. You still have the stink of swamp in you, and yet," she pulled a lank of hair, "the woman returns."

"Release me, I've done you no harm."

"No harm? Is my skin smooth as silk?" She pulled her closer, allowing Catherine to see the wrinkles cascading across her face. "No harm? Is my body the suppleness of womanhood?" She yanked her sleeve back.

"The fault is yours. You tied yourself to the curse." Catherine struggled to free herself. How strong had the witch been if her body was now weakened by age?

The witch snarled. "I am not the one to blame in all of this. You let some weak-bellied charmer talk you into kissing him."

Catherine gasped. "I'd rather have a kind heart that mistakenly trusts, then no heart at all."

Something, someone came running toward them. Catherine shrieked as a large body barreled into them, throwing all to the ground. She rolled from the witch's grasp.

Catherine gasped. "Rorry." How had he found them?

"Rodrick?" The witch seemed just as surprised. Her cackle echoed across the pond. "Is that you, dear boy? Grown into a man?" Her voice turned dark. "Is this your idea of revenge?"

Rorry jumped to his feet. "I tried to talk her into kissing me, but she wouldn't have it."

"What would you have done then?" The old woman's face twisted in a snarl. "Sacrifice yourself, all to get back at poor little me?"

"It's time to stop hurting people, destroying their lives."

Catherine stayed on the ground, turning from one to the other. She should run, but the play between the two held her captive.

The witch brushed dirt from her sleeve. "I expected my son to follow in my footsteps."

Rorry straightened. "I am not your son."

"Truly? Was it not I who raised you? Provided shelter, food, even affection when you craved it?"

"You stole me from my family." His fists clenched at his sides.

"Semantics boy." She waved her hand and then turned cold eyes on Catherine. "This one is more trouble than she is worth. We are well rid of her."

With the cold eyes of the witch fully on her once more, Catherine realized her mistake in remaining. She scurried back, but the aging witch was fast, stronger than most even in her weakened state. She nabbed Catherine's ankle, and Catherine could not shake her loose.

"Why did you follow us?" Catherine implored Rorry as she fought against the witch's grasp. "Do you mean to help her or to help me?"

"He'll wait until it's too late to decide," the witch cackled again as she stretched her other hand to grasp Catherine's throat.

Catherine fought against the weight pressing down on her, digging her nails into the witch's arm. A low growl emanated from the older woman, increasing in volume until the witch hurled herself away. The scent of burning flesh hovered a moment before wafting across the water. Catherine scrambled back. What had happened? Rorry offered a hand to pull her to her feet, and then he pushed her behind him.

"Go. Return to the village. Find our rooms and lock yourself in."

"Do you believe a locked door could separate us? Or have you used a little spell?" The witch stood, shaking her head as she rubbed her arms. "Foolish Rorry, there is no strength in dabbling."

"I have never desired your kind of strength."

"Of course not. You were too good for the life I offered." The witch rushed toward him. Too late, Catherine realized the gleam that caught her eye was a weapon. Rorry stepped into it.

With a cry, Catherine felt Rorry's body stiffen. She heard the sound of the knife being pulled from flesh. With her arms wrapped around his chest, she fell to the ground with him.

"Always a price for meddling," the witch's voice cracked as though pained by the turn of events. With the knife still grasped in her hand, she raised her arm. Catherine buried her head against Rorry, unable to flee, unable to protect herself or him from the blow to come. Her body stiffened, but just a swish of air moved across her skin. Time seemed to still. Finally, she peeked, sat up, and looked around. The witch was gone. Starlight gleamed across the pond. The insects began their chirping harmony once more. What had happened? She pulled away from Rorry. He moaned.

"Rorry," Catherine pressed against his chest until his painful cry made her jerk back.

He moved his hands to his side. "A flesh wound," he gasped, "not fatal I think."

She grabbed the blanket at her side, then realized her clothes had changed. She looked down. "My dress, the dress I wore when first I met Andy." What did it mean?

"The spell completely unwound." He tried to sit up, but she pushed his shoulder.

"Don't move, what if you do more harm?" She tore one of the petticoats free and handed the material to him. "Press this against the wound. We must stop the bleeding before we try returning to the village."

"Careful, Catherine, you sound like you might care."

"I don't wish you dead." Exasperating man.

"Nor do I wish death upon you." He closed his eyes and winced as he pressed the cloth against the wound. "Mayhap we should keep each other close for safety's sake."

He joked, didn't he? Such a thing wouldn't do. Not for her, and not for him. So why did her heart flutter at the thought?

Thank you for reading my first collection of fairytales. The next collection, *Twice Upon a Time in Fairyland*, will bring even more wonderful tales of magical realms, princes and princesses, and of course faeries. Until then, here's a list of other stories by Laurie Lee to enjoy.

- Cinderella Spell (fantasy)
- Legends: Within the Dark Realm (fantasy)

Ready for more fairytales? Continue through to read the beginning of a dark tale, Wolf and the Girl in the Red Cloak.

Laurie Lee is the fantasy penname for author Laurie Boulden. Enjoy these other selections by Laurie.

- Sisters of Mercy House Gardens: Lilly and that Nice Detective (suspense)
- Sisters of Mercy House Gardens: Astra and that Handsome Bachelor (contemporary romance)
- Hidden Gems (suspense)
- By the Fruit of Her Hands: Jewel of Jericho (Biblical fiction)
- By the Fruit of Her Hands: Mistress of Moab (Biblical fiction)
- By the Fruit of Her Hands: Pearl of Persia (Biblical fiction)
- By the Fruit of Her Hands: Journeying the Walls of Jericho (Biblical devotion)

- [Cookies, Cocoa, and Capers](#) (Christmas rom com)
- [Her Christmas Misfortune](#) (Christmas rom com)
- [A Time to Die](#) (time travel suspense)
- [The Cat from Camden Place](#) (suspense with a touch of fantasy)
- [Cowboy Blessing](#) (sweet romance)
- [The Maxwell Murders](#) (suspense)
- [Flood: A Wife for Shem](#) (Biblical Fiction)

Connect with author Laurie Boulden:

- [On Facebook](#)
- [On Instagram](#)
- [On Twitter](#)
- [Website](#)

Wolf and the Girl in the Red Cloak

Beams of light flitted through the overhanging branches heavy with leaves. Nary a bird chirped, or summer locust hummed through the trees. Sabine slowed her steps as she noticed light splashing across the weathered overhang of an ancient house. "Chrissy," she whispered, as the hush of the woods settled across her shoulders like a scratchy blanket. Her older sister, several feet ahead as usual, turned on the path to face her. Sabine pointed. "Who would build this deep into the forest?"

Chrissy's face brightened. "Grandmother's house." She skipped across a patch of moss.

Sabine shook her head. "We shouldn't be here Chrissy." Though a chill touched the air, she felt flush, drawn and yet repelled by the Victorian shelter. With its sharp angled roof, the house fit between two great trees. Ornate lintels of deep blue hung beneath the gable, with matching spindles across the porch. Thin clapboards had faded to gray, and moss clung to cracked slate shingles. Present and yet abandoned. A relic of an older age.

Chrissy didn't seem to notice. Her eyes shone when she grabbed Sabine's hand. "Grandmother lived here. Not right, that you would find it when she was my grandmother." She squeezed.

Sabine pulled her hand back. "What do you mean, your grandmother? We're sisters. She'd be my grandmother as well." She looked at the house. "And how do you know this is her place? I've never heard of it."

"My grandmother belongs to my father." Chrissy tugged her closer to the porch. "Your father didn't have a mother anymore."

Sabine dug her heels into the soft dirt forming a path to the entrance. "Stop it, Chrissy. You aren't funny."

But Chrissy wouldn't let go. She tugged Sabine to the foot of the stairs. "My father was killed by bandits as he traveled home from a festival far away. Grandmother couldn't bear the news. She died right there, in front of mother and me. Mother dragged me away and we haven't been here since. She moved to town and met your father a year later."

"He's our father, Chrissy." Sabine tasted bile choking her. "I don't like this, I want to go home."

"Not yet." The normally calm and fearless Chrissy pleaded, her eyes sad. "The house is here. Like I remember it, but older. I had a doll. A tiny thing with blonde hair and porcelain skin." Chrissy's eyes filled with tears. Sabine gulped her own, but she couldn't walk away. Chrissy pressed her hand. "Please, Sabine." Her voice was a whisper. "She should be there, if what I remember is true." A single tear dripped from her lashes and coursed down her cheek. "But I can't go in there. Grandmother... but you never knew Grandmother. The house holds no memories for you. Please, Sabine, if you've ever loved me. Please find my doll. At least try."

She didn't want to. Not one ounce of herself wanted to step onto the porch, let alone through the front door that gaped open. The afternoon remained bright, but the forest hid more shadows. She stepped onto the first riser. Her heart quickened, her mind begging her to run in the other direction. But she couldn't, not with Chrissy urging her to the next step. Her feet moved, and she stood on the worn boards of the porch, watching dried and shriveled leaves brush across her shoes.

With the door open, she could see into the house. Large windows provided light, so she could make out a tall table, broken chair, a stone fireplace against a far wall.

"Just a few more steps, Sabine. Please, for me? I promise I won't tease you anymore. You'll be braver than me."

She wasn't brave, but neither could she turn back.

Something changed as she crossed the threshold into the wide kitchen. The hairs on the back of her neck stood out. Her hand opened and she dropped the willow branch she'd been carrying all morning. Her body tingled, and then waves of pain rolled from her feet, up her legs, through her back, and over her head. She felt as though she bent double, yet she seemed unable to move. Unable to scream though her voice rattled in her throat. Her hands grew larger, longer. Indentations between her knuckles deepened. Her supple skin stretched, brownish spots appearing as its color faded to clear. She stretched a wrinkling hand toward Chrissy, but her mind started to gray. Her lips forgot the words pressing against her heart. Weakness pained her legs, and she fell to the stone floor.

"Do be careful, Grandmother." The young girl outside the door hollered.

Sabine grinned, waved a gnarled hand at her. "It's okay, dear. Tell your mother hello. So kind of you to visit." *Floor needs sweeping.* She patted the dust with a sigh. *Tired these days. Very tired. And weak.* She crawled to the stool beneath the counter and used it to pull herself to her feet. She looked down with a frown. Odd shoes for an old woman.